Just Sippy

Just Sippy

KIMBERLY J. COLEMAN

Silverbell Publishing

Published by
Silverbell Publishing
P.O. Box 669
Johnstown, Colorado 80534
info@silverbellpublishing.com

www.justsippy.com

ISBN: 978-0-578-07798-7

Author photograph by Graham Photography
Zapata's Horse: The Book of While, Copyright © 2003 Joseph H.
Coleman. Characters and events used with permission from the
author.

Printed in the United States of America

This story is dedicated to
Adam, Nick, Jessica, Jennifer, Jonathan,
Xander, Jenna, and Natalie

ACKNOWLEDGMENTS

T is fitting to start at the beginning and thank my parents; all four of them.

Thanks to my dad, Joe, for always being proud, and for sharing your love of words and music. I am honored to have that part of you in me.

And to my mom, Diane, first, for marrying my dad and second, for picking up the pieces each time my world has fallen apart, I love you. (See, I love you for more than just Kraft Spaghetti)

To my mom, Judy, thanks for always challenging me, teaching me to be independent, and believing that I would do this someday. I love you more. (HA!) You owe me some Chop Suey, by the way.

And to Daddy-I miss you. Thank you for marrying mom. And, I hear ya, "Very Good!"

A big thank you goes to my sister, Cindy, for leaving that snotty little child behind and becoming one of my favorite women. Just for being you; my sister and my friend, I love you.

To A.H. and D.P., thank you for putting up with the teen version of me. I have never forgotten you.

To my friends who took this journey with Sippy, over and over and over. I think it is time for some bottom bouncers, karaoke and Sangria! And yes, all at the same time.

To the three men in my life-thanks for making me strong, determined, and free!

Thanks to my children, who have made my life so joyous. Thank you for the laughter, the silliness, and the smiles. I love you all more than anything. This is for you.

To those who made me a Power Ranger and to my fellow Power Rangers…best time of my life!

To my dear friend, Kevin-First copy is yours just like I promised.

To Linda, my personal gift from God, I am proud to call you my friend. I will tell the story of our friendship until the day I die. It truly is amazing!

To my publisher, Silverbell Publishing, there are no words to express my gratitude.

And, finally, to my "Jilly", you know who you are. I love you so much and you made this happen.

And you are right, this is not the end.

PROLOGUE

NEVER have been good at tellin' stories. Mama says I talk too fast, and Daddy says I leave out important stuff like the color the sky was or how the room smelled. I just tell it, is all—the way I see it. Guess I don't notice the sky much. And all I ever smell is fish. Damn river. Every time it rains, I can't smell nothin' but fish.

Most folks don't notice that smell no more, but I do. And most folks have lived here their whole lives. Even their mama and daddy and granddad and memaw have lived here their whole lives. Memaw. That's what I call my grandmother. Don't know why. Never did hear that story. Guess I should of asked. Probably wouldn't tell it right though, so it don't really matter none.

I got a better story to tell. It don't matter if I tell it right or not. Ain't nobody gonna hear it but you. And nobody else is gonna tell it. So it's just 'tween you and me. Now, if I get goin' too fast, well, I'm mighty sorry. If I forget to tell ya a smell or a color, just make one up in yer head. I don't think color matters none, but the sky here is blue like anyplace else. And like I said, all ya ever smell is fish.

My name's Sippy. That's not my given name, of

1

course. When I tell ya my real name, ya can't laugh. I got two memaws, and Mama and Daddy wanted me named after 'em, but they couldn't choose one over the other for my first name, so I got two middle names, Bernice and GraceAnna.

Have I told ya yet my daddy loves storytellin', fables, and anything odd or unusual? Have ya ever heard of The Three Princes of Serendip or Horace Walpole? I'm not surprised none if ya haven't. From what I gather, there is a fairy tale about some princes who found stuff by accident and whatnot. Well, them princes, they was from Serendip (that's a country), and they made a real big impression on that Walpole guy. So he made up a word—serendipity — to mean "by accident."

My daddy said I came to them by accident. So he named me—no laughin' now—Serendipity! Serendipity Bernice GraceAnna Johnson. But try teachin' that to a baby brother. It comes out Sippy. And that's what everybody calls me. Just Sippy.

I got two brothers and two sisters. They got normal names—Thomas Joseph, Rebecca Elizabeth, Emma Ruth, and the baby, James Scott. Of course, to us, they's Tommy, Becky, Emmy, and Jimmy. Two is older and two is younger. I fit right in the middle. And we got a dog. We call him Whiskey. He's almost eleven, which is how old I am. Daddy says he ain't gonna make it much longer. Hope he never says that about me. I guess in dog years, though, eleven is a lot. That's what Becky told me anyhow. She tells me a lot of the stuff I don't know.

She told me about our neighbor, old Mr. Baker. Guess he's not really mean like we all thought. He's just sad. His wife had an operation years ago, and she couldn't have babies. So they just stayed alone all their life. When she passed, summer before last, he just got sad. I always heard he was a mean old man and not to go near his gate or he'd come after ya with a chain saw. I never have walked that way home. My friend Max don't believe Becky and says he's as mean as all the stories say. Says it's all true, and he's seen the saw even.

"Seen it with my own eyes. Hangin' in the shed when me and Pa did some work for him."

"That don't mean nothin'," I told him. "Daddy's got a saw himself."

But he said Mr. Baker's had blood all over it.

"Drippin' right down into his hay bales!"

I didn't believe him none. I think he just likes to show off. He does that a lot. Becky says it's 'cause he is smitten with me, but I don't think she's right about that at all. Max is just a boy, and boys love to show off.

Becky also told me about the curse I'll be gettin' soon. All girls get it, she said. She said it will come every month with the full moon, and it's women's punishment for what Eve did. I said Memaw never told me anything about that when she taught me about the Bible. I said I never heard such nonsense, but she swears it's true. Becky wouldn't swear if it weren't true.

Now mind ya, nothin' real excitin' ever happens around here. We live in Iowa, and well, it's just like you heard it to be. Quiet. Everybody knows everybody. We don't have dirt floors, and we aren't married to our cousins like the jokes say. Although Daddy says Mama's crazy friend, Dottie Roberts, and her husband Frank are related on her Mama's side.

"It sure would explain a lot about them kids o' theirs." That's what Daddy said to Mama, and then he reminded her about a time when them kids was on top of their house and they just started jumpin' off it. "Two of 'em broke their arms, and I think they all got stitches somewhere. They said they was tryin' to fly!" Then Mama remembered a time those kids were makin' tents out of blankets.

"Remember? They had one side tucked behind the davenport, and the other side was over a chair. One of them thought it looked like a trampoline and jumped off the back of the davenport right into the middle of that stretched-out blanket." Mama put her hands on her hips and spun around to face Daddy. "Frank's mama was sittin' there. Remember me tellin' ya? She was holdin' that blanket in place. Why, it flipped that poor woman right clean outta that chair." She shook her head. "Looked like a turtle on it's back when she tried gettin' up."

Mama said she was darn mad at those kids. She chased after 'em, but they just ran off gigglin'. Daddy says all them kids are still pretty wild.

Since our town is so small, we hear lots of stories like that, and usually the people are some relation to a neighbor or two. So let me tell ya. When something big does happen, it's the talk all right. And somebody always manages to know your business. I ain't figured out yet how that happens, but it does.

My brother, Tommy, skipped school once with Mary Beth Lawrence. He took her down to the river for a picnic, way down on the island side where no one lives or has any reason to be, and I'll be darned if Daddy didn't hear about it down in Bakers Flatt, about thirty miles from here. And he knowed it long before they even got done eatin' the pie Mary Beth stole from her grandmother's kitchen. Shoot, her grandmother didn't even know the pie was gone, and the whole town knew they ate it.

My Aunt Lily found out she was gonna be havin' my cousin Billy from the lady at the beauty shop. Mama said the nurse at the doctor's office was the sister-in-law of one of the ladies who fixes hair, and she spilled the beans. Becky told me eatin' beans won't make me with child; I was glad to hear that, 'cause I hadn't ate beans in a long time.

Like I said, I'm eleven, which makes it 1973. And my story starts in November.

I had stayed late at school to help my teacher, Miss Allen, get ready for Thanksgiving. I usually walk home with Emmy, who is nine and bossy, and Jimmy, who is seven. For some reason, he'd started being mad all the time. They fight somethin' terrible, so I didn't mind walkin' alone. I like time by myself. I sing. I think. And I listen. Did you know you can listen to the quiet? I like it.

Our weather was unusually warm. It was a nice, quiet walk. I was thinkin' about Miss Allen and all her funny turkey cutouts. She was determined to hang them all over the ceiling. She had the kindergarten kids color them as an extra project. She said when a good breeze came through the windows, it would look like they were flyin'. She is so silly. But it made me laugh out loud when I thought of her standin' on her steppin' stool with all them flyin' rainbow-colored turkeys.

I must have only walked another five minutes or so when, all of a sudden, the wind started blowin', and all the clouds darkened up, and the temperature must have dropped ten degrees! We wasn't fixin' to have any storms I knew of. But my hair was every which way, and I could barely see where I was goin'.

The treetops were rubbin' against each other, and they were makin' quite a roar. I started thinkin' about the weatherman saying it'd be clear and sunny for the next two days, and then it stopped. Just as quick as it come up, the wind was gone, and it was still as could be. The darkness turned back to light, and it was warm again.

The goose pimples on my arms was gone, and my hair layed soft again outta my eyes. The leaves quit blowin' across the road. The trees were quiet. I must have turned in circles for a good twenty feet. I went forwards and backwards, lookin' every which way. I looked up, but the sky didn't have a cloud in it. It was just as blue as could be. (Daddy would be proud of me for that.)

I stopped at the start of our road and sat my books down on an old tree stump. I looked back and wondered what kind of storm that was. Miss Allen taught us about the weather last year, but I didn't remember anything about just wind.

Our road has the creek on one side and the back of Mr. Baker's farm on the other. It made me kind of wonder about Mr. Baker and what Becky said. But I knew Becky wouldn't lie about that, so I didn't wonder long. I stood up, gathered my books, and continued home. I started thinkin' how hungry I was gettin', and I hoped Mama was puttin' on some supper. Biscuits sounded real good. I was hopin' for biscuits.

Our road is more like a lane, and it doesn't take a hot second to get to the house. Mama was in the kitchen when I walked in the back door. She was yellin' at Tommy to keep his things outside. Apparently, just before I got there, she had tripped over his fishing rod and tackle box and spilled a whole bucket of flour right down her front.

I stopped long enough to giggle just a bit and ran on up to my room. Becky was in her room listenin' to the radio, and Emmy and Jimmy was fightin' over something that happened in the lunchroom.

I figured Daddy was downstairs workin' on one of his projects. He is always tinkerin' around with something in the basement. He is like an inventor, only he doesn't make new things. He tries to prove things that already exist don't work right or could work better. I guess sometimes he does invent things, but it's mostly by accident. That's the serendipity in him.

One time, we were all sittin' around doing our homework when every light we had went out. Even the ones outside on the porch went black. Mama looked out, and all the neighbors down the road was in the dark too. We all knew Daddy must have done somethin', so we went to the basement door. Sure enough, there he was, and he was covered from head to toe in what looked like blue food coloring.

"Oh, Jack! What have you—" Mama started to ask him.

"Just get me a flashlight, Suzie," he told her. "I can't see a thing down here."

Long story short, the service men from the electric company had to come out and fix the main breaker. Daddy was told he couldn't be messin' with the electricity no more.

He said he was tryin' to figure out a way to automatically get those blue toilet things into the commode.

"'Cause ya buy 'em, and then ya forget to put a new one in."

Mama just shook her head, and since Daddy don't know about electric stuff, he had somethin' hooked up way wrong. Caused a big power surge in the whole east side of town. Not to mention, he blew up all ten of those little things. I thought the basement smelled real good for a long time, but Mama said she couldn't stand the smell of 'em after that, and she never bought another one.

I went into my room and closed the door. I sat my books down. I thought about the walk home. I knew there were tornadoes all the time, but they weren't in the winter, and I felt like I was the only one who felt it. Not a soul was talkin' about it. Not a one of 'em asked me about it. I started wishin' someone else had been there. At least there would have been a witness. Even if Emmy and Jimmy was fightin', they'd have felt it. I just wished someone else was there so they could tell me I wasn't crazy. And right then, was the first time he spoke. And all he said was, "You're not crazy."

CHAPTER ONE

Now, I'm sure I don't have to tell ya how high I jumped. I don't have to give specific details about how my face must have looked or how big my eyeballs got or even about the water that welled up in 'em. I don't have to tell ya any of that, 'cause I'm sure you can figure out for yourself that it scared the you-know-what outta me!

We aren't churchgoin' people like Memaw, so I'm not in real good with the man upstairs. We're not on a first name basis, anyway. So I didn't for one minute think it was Him talkin' to me. But I sure was callin' out His name. And it was in vain, if I got Mama's meaning of that right in my head. But you can bet I was yellin' it.

After a while, I calmed down a bit, but it was just a bit, mind ya. I was still breathing as if I'd run a mile or two, and some sweat was tricklin' down my upper lip. I eased over to the door, and then I ran like heck all the way down the steps and through the livin' room. Then I ran through the dinin' room, into the kitchen, and straight out the back door. I heard blips and blurbs of my name being called out, but I was runnin' so fast, I was gone before the name came all the way out of their mouths!

In the back of our house is a stream—runoff from nearby Dyers Creek—that separates our back yard from a hill we call Johnson Mountain. Unlike most of the land around our house, Johnson Mountain isn't owned by anybody that I know of. The woods at the top lead down to gully where the city sewer system starts.

It ain't gross or nothin' down in there. It's just real quiet. Nobody goes there but us kids, with it bein' the start of the sewer and all. I like to go there and think, so I ran through our yard, jumped our mini-creek, scurried up the mountain, and ran into the woods.

In the gully, I sat there on an old tree that had been knocked down three or four summers ago during a big lightning storm. It was a big ol' tree, and truth be known, it would have quite the story to tell. I sat there thinkin' about absolutely nothin'.

I wasn't thinkin' about walkin' home or Miss Allen's turkeys. I wasn't thinkin' about Mama or Daddy. I wasn't thinkin' about school or old Mr. Baker. I wasn't even thinkin' about being hungry or the fact I had to pee. But I especially wasn't thinkin' about what just happened in my room.

Mama used to tell me if I was having a hard time sleepin' or if I had a bad dream, I should just close my eyes and try to see something beautiful. It could be a place I wanted to go or somewhere I'd already been that I liked.

So I sat there on that old tree and took my mama's advice. I thought of butterflies flittin' through a beautiful field. I imagined fields of golden wheat, soft and free-flowin'. That wheat looked so soft in my mind. I almost felt a tickle on my nose. I brushed the invisible away. Then I thought of blue and purple flowers. And pink and yellow, too. I could smell something sweet as I thought of them. Lavender. I smelled lavender.

Listen to me. All of a sudden, I'm describin' colors and a smell—a smell other than fish, that is. Then I smelled it. Fish! Even without it rainin', I smelled fish. Some things never change. I heard Tommy callin' my name, and I knew I had to go home. They was all gonna be askin' what my hurry was. But I didn't want what happened in my room to be the subject at the supper table. One time when Becky was little, she thought she saw a ghost in the backyard, and the whole family thought she was crazy.

Well, Daddy didn't. But like I already told ya, Daddy liked the strange and unusual. So he was quite happy about it. Everybody else just thought she was nuts. Tommy called for me again. I hollered back and headed through the woods to the top of Johnson Mountain. Tommy was at the bottom on the other side of the stream.

He was waving his hands all over the place. I waved back, but then I realized he was swattin' at the most beautiful butterflies I had ever seen. It was the oddest sight. There were big ones, small ones, orange ones, and yellow ones. Some were rich black against bright orange. Some were a deeper black that was almost blue. I had never seen such a thing. Not even in my imagination had there been so many.

As I watched him, the butterflies fluttered away.

Without lookin' back at me, Tommy told me it was time for supper. As I walked down the side of our mountain and jumped over our mini-creek, I saw a bunch of wildflowers growin' along the side of our house. We never had any kind of flowers growin' there before. I couldn't make out what kind they were, but the pink and yellow ones were the brightest I had ever seen.

Now here it was, the beginning of November, and I was seeing flowers and butterflies, and I was hearing voices talk to me. Right then, I realized I wasn't gonna say a word about any of this to anybody. Some things are just better left unsaid.

I could tell Tommy was annoyed Mama made him come after me. As soon as I made myself visible, he ran off the same way he came. I made it back up to the house and entered our kitchen through our back door. Mama had dinner all ready. Us kids set the table. Becky talked about a new boy in school.

"Oh, Mama. He's so nice, and his eyes are real pretty. His daddy is a business man, and they just moved here from Chicago, I think. His Mama has her own makeup company and everything!"

Jimmy and Emmy were still fighting over the lunchroom incident.

"He did so do it on purpose!" Emmy screamed. "And we all went to Mr. Alexander and said he should get kicked right outta school!" She continued, and Jimmy tried to speak. She interrupted.

"Probably ruined her new skirt, gettin' milk spilled all over it like that!" Emmy wasn't letting up.

It seemed Matthew Walker threw a carton of milk, and it spilled all over a girl's clothes. Jimmy said he didn't mean to splash the girl, but Emmy insisted it was on purpose.

There are so many unsolved arguments between those two. They still argue over who broke the antenna off the television and whether or not Mr. Ed really talks. One day last week they fought 'cause Emmy threw a shoe, and it hit Jimmy in the leg.

"You did so! You threw a shoe at my leg. Right here!" Jimmy pointed to the red part of his calf.

"No, I didn't," Emmy screamed back.

"Yes you did!" He pointed again.

"No. I threw it at your head!" She marched away as if she was the winner. Can you even settle an agreement like that? I smiled at the thought while I listened to their current disagreement fadin' out. We sat down to dinner, and they stopped their bickerin'. It wasn't allowed at the table.

Over supper, Daddy mentioned to Mama that Brighton River Days was coming up.

"There's a new contest this year, Suze. Best home-made recipes." He nodded toward Mama. "You know you got the best sweet potato pie for forty miles."

We all agreed.

Mama made biscuits and gravy. It was my favorite supper, but hungry as I'd been, I could only manage one helping. Daddy asked how Miss Allen was doing and how school was coming along. Tommy asked if he could go fishing the whole weekend with the Pratt boys. Daddy said no.

"It's winter, son. Ain't fit for fishin'. Ya'll can wait 'til spring."

"But the weather's like spring out." I thought for sure Tommy would argue and mention seeing all those butterflies, but he didn't. Nobody asked why I had run off so fast. I was glad 'cause I wouldn't have known what to say. Mama told Tommy to let it be and wait 'til spring like Daddy said.

After supper, Becky and me did the cleanin' up. She washed the dishes, while I scrubbed down the stove and the table. She was goin' on and on about that new boy, Aaron Waters. She thought it was neat he had the same name as Elvis. I made a joke about his name being Elvis the Pelvis, but Becky didn't think it was funny. Tommy sure did. He laughed out loud, and then Becky hollered that we should have to apologize.

Mama just shook her head and raised her eyebrows at us. That was our cue to stop harassing Becky. Why do parents take the fun out of everything? Most parents do, anyway. Daddy doesn't do that, though, and that night was no different.

He was doing another one of his silly experiments. He had two exact copies of an Ernest Hemingway book. He had one in each hand, and he was sure they weighed different amounts.

"I mean it, now. They weigh different. I think I am absorbin' up the knowledge outta this one." Daddy held one book open. "Come on, Suzie. You do it!"

But she wouldn't.

"Certain to make me look a fool, aren't you, Jack?"

Mama folded her arms across her chest in protest and walked away from Daddy. "And it's a waste of money to buy a book ya already have."

Daddy disagreed and told Mama she wasn't any fun. He was just teasin'. He loved her, and you could tell.

You could always tell what Daddy loved. He had a certain smile that would come across his face when he loved somethin'. And you saw it anytime he talked about Mama, baseball, or music. Like Buddy Holly.

"A legendary rock singer in horn-rimmed glasses," Daddy described him once. "Took from this life too soon. A plane crash up in Clear Lake. Right here in Iowa."

He must have been a big deal, though, 'cause a guy just last year sang a song about him on the radio. He said it was the day the music died. I know it made Daddy real sad, but he still smiled that special smile when he talked about him or his music. It was just like when he talked about Mama. Or baseball.

Daddy and I used to go up to the park in town and play baseball every Sunday.

"Battin' stance and pitchin' technique is still important, Sip. Even for a girl," he said as we walked onto the field one day. We was playin' one-on-one, and I had smacked the ball pretty good. The sun was all up in Daddy's eyes, so I got ahead. He tried one more time to catch up, but I struck him out. Daddy always let me take a victory lap.

Daddy waited for me on the bench by the dugout. Some big shots from the park's department were talkin' to him about raisin' funds for the new Little League park. Daddy loved talkin' to folks about stuff like that.

"It's important for the kids to have a nice place to go. You boys need to come down when there's a game and watch 'em play. Them boys. They's all real good," Daddy told the man with pride.

"You got a great little ball player there. How old is he?" the man asked as he pointed to me. I took my baseball cap off just then, and my long hair fell to the middle of my back. He realized his mistake.

"Oh, I'm sorr—" He tried to apologize, but Daddy stopped him.

"Yes, she is good. She's six," Daddy said, and I saw that smile. The one he smiles when he looks at Mama. Or talks about music. Or baseball.

I never wore that hat again. I don't really know why. I just didn't. I started spendin' time in my room, and I discovered reading. Daddy started spendin' Sundays in the basement. Sometimes I join him, and we talk about books. And baseball.

And I still see that smile now and again. I saw it that night in the way he looked at Mama. And Mama is happy, even though she just shakes her head at Daddy as if he is one of us. She loves him right back.

Becky noticed I was bein' kind of quiet outside of my Elvis comment, but I told her I was just thinkin' about a test at school, and I really wanted to hurry to go study. She believed me. I didn't like lyin' to her, but I knew I couldn't tell her the truth. I didn't even know the truth.

Oh yeah. And then this voice told me I wasn't crazy, I thought to myself. Just thinkin' it made me shiver a bit. I wondered again if I was goin' crazy. I stopped to look over my shoulder when I thought that. I was sure some big, scary man would be standin' there shakin' his finger at me as if to say, "Oh no you don't, missy! Don't you be thinkin' that way."

Just the thought made me shiver again. Becky didn't notice. She was too busy fixin' her hair in the window above the sink.

Becky's got the prettiest hair I've ever seen in real life, besides Mama's, that is. Like Mama, Becky's hair is dark brown, and it looks like it has tiny little lights in it. Sometimes I watch her when she brushes it, and I try to brush mine the same exact way. But mine don't shimmer like hers.

She wears it real long, and it has a natural wave in it. She never has to use rollers or get a permanent. It just does it all on its own. Mine is straight as a board and lighter. I figure I get my hair from Daddy. I don't really know, though, since most of his hair has been gone for a long time.

I watched Becky for a while. Her eyes were dark like her hair, but tonight they seemed lighter. They weren't pale like mine, but they were lighter than their normal color. Daddy says Becky's eyes are the color of chestnuts. I suppose that's a good thing, since he says it so sweet-like.

I hadn't seen her smitten like this since the summer before last when the River Boat Carnival was here. She waited over an hour outside the

Mirror House for Ronnie Pratt to get off work. He was workin' Thursday nights and Sunday afternoons tryin' to earn enough money to take Becky on a date.

He said he was savin' every dime so he could do her right. Carnival work must not pay too good 'cause when they went on their date, he just took her to the Dairy Mart up on the highway. She wasn't too happy about it, but she pretended to be.

I didn't think it sounded too bad. He let her get a shake. But then I don't know nothin' about dates since I ain't never been on one. I think they sound kind of dumb. I mean, what's the big deal, anyway? It's just food, and everybody has to eat. My friend Max and I eat together all the time, and it's no big deal. Becky says it will be someday, when I am older.

After we were done cleanin', I went up to my room. I opened the door real slow. Lookin' all around, I didn't see a thing out of the ordinary. There was no big, scary man shakin' his finger at me.

Like I said, we are not churchgoin', but we do believe in God. I went to Bible school once when I was little, and I've learned stuff from Memaw, so I know all the basics.

I didn't think people actually heard a real voice, though.

Once, when Memaw was entertainin', she told her friends about the church fundraiser comin' up, and I heard one of the ladies say, "The Heavenly Father spoke to me and told me to tithe more."

And later, when Memaw assured one lady she was missed at services, the lady replied, "The Lord has been telling me to get to church, but my arthritis bothers me so in the morning."

Still, I never thought those were real voices. I just figured they were kind of like thoughts. The voice part had me real confused. That being said, I thought I better play it safe. I figured I better get in good with the man upstairs. After all, if He was the one talkin', I wouldn't wanna be ignorin' him and all. That I knew for sure. So in my room that night, I had my first real talk with God.

"God? It's me, Sippy. Oh, you already know that. Well, here's the deal. If that was you who spoke to me … or any of your partners up there … you know, the Saints or one of the Wise Men … well, that's OK, too.

"In fact, if you authorized anyone, that is OK. I get it. It's just, well, from now on, can ya just send me a sign? I really didn't like the voice. Not the voice itself. If it was you, it's a real nice voice. But, well, the idea of the voice. You know, the actual sound. Well, uh … I would really prefer, from now on, if you didn't really talk. Something quiet will be just fine. Just a sign.

"You know, knock a picture over or turn a faucet on. Somethin' like that. I like the communication, don't get me wrong. I love that part, but next time I will just take a sign."

I stopped brief then and decided to add, "And while I have you listenin', can you make it look like winter around here? It's all warm and more like spring. We really need some winter weather to make us feel festive. After all, Thanksgiving is comin', and it feels more like Easter. Nothin' drastic, just … chill it up a bit, OK? Okay." I answered myself to avoid an actual reply.

Then I quickly added, "Thanks."

I nodded and waved a little to formally excuse myself.

I felt better with that out of the way, and since I really did have studyin' to do, I got my math out. I chose it first since I wasn't great in English. I love readin' books and all, but writin' is not my thing. Miss Allen says I write like I talk, and she isn't thrilled about it at all.

"It's lazy English, boys and girls. It's why some people believe people from around here aren't smart," she told our class.

I didn't get that at all. Heck, I don't think anybody's dumb. Well, OK, maybe one. But it's not 'cause of how he talks. His name is Scotty McDaniels, and he is dumb.

In second grade, I was sittin' in front of him, and he dipped my ponytail right down into his blue art paint. 'Course I didn't know it until we was all outside, and a group of kids started callin' me a blue-back whale. I was fixin' to go after him and show him what I was made of, but my friend Max stopped me. I should have punched him later in the hall when no one was lookin'.

Mama was mad, too, when I come home from school with a big spot of blue paint all down my school shirt. He had to come to our house three Saturdays in a row to work off the cost of replacing it.

Another time, when the whole class was goin'

out to the Pratt Farm on a hayrack ride, he thought it would be funny to set off a bunch of firecrackers right next to the horses pullin' the hayrack. Luckily, he stuck 'em in the hay too far. All it did was make a big mess all over.

Teacher said them horses would have taken off for the whole day if the sound hadn't been muffled like it was. It took the adults a good hour to get that hay to stop smolderin'. The principal just called his mama, and he had to go home for the day.

We heard his daddy was gonna send him away to military school. He never played another prank, so the threat must have been true. Now he is just big and dumb, and he's always askin' to carry my books and buy me extra milk at lunch. He must think I'm a wimp and that we are poor or somethin'.

After math, I worked on my science. I was gonna look up butterflies and see if they are ever around in November, but decided I didn't wanna know. I only remembered seeing them in the summer, and I decided it must have been some kind of winter moth I saw. Maybe I imagined the butterflies. If they were real, Tommy sure would have used them in his argument to go fishin'.

The Pratt boys were gonna be fishin' all weekend out at Charlotte's Cove. It's about six miles outside of town on Highway 34, and it goes on for miles and miles. There is so much timber that one person could never get through it in a lifetime. There are campin' sites and a swimmin' hole. The trails leading up into the woods go on and on. The county has put a lot of money into makin' it a learnin' experience. They've marked the trees with ID tags so you know what you are lookin' at. Even some of the smaller bushes and flowers have little name markers. The school takes us there on field trips every year.

There is a rock quarry too, where the water has carved through the rocks. One spot looks just like a cat with a ball of yarn, and another looks like a fish in a net.

Mama says they change every hundred years or so, but I don't know how she'd know that. Have you ever noticed how mamas know stuff that people normally don't know? Like my mama. She knows all the phone numbers to stores all over town. She even knows ones in other towns to places she don't never go. There must be a book or something that gives 'em all that know-how.

I was finishin' up the definitions of my science words when Becky came in my room. She was still smilin' about that new boy at school.

"Mama says to be sure to wear a coat tomorrow. There's a cold front movin' in." She turned away but stopped and turned back. "Oh, and if you spill her lavender perfume again, just clean it up."

She bounced out of the room just as quick as she'd come in.

I thought about the cold front and just looked up at the ceilin'. It was Him. He heard me! He really heard me. It didn't matter I didn't spill Mama's perfume. I knew He did.

CHAPTER TWO

OVER the next few days, a cold front did come in, and it brought with it four inches of snow. Tommy's job was gettin' our road plowed out, and he even went over and helped Mr. Baker with his.

I really do think Becky is right about Mr. Baker; I don't think he is mean at all. Poor Tommy wouldn't have made it out alive if the stories were true. Miss Allen had given us a big assignment to start over Thanksgiving break, and the weatherman had forecasted more snow, so I knew our holiday would be real busy.

We were busy cleanin' and preparin' for our Thanksgiving dinner, and like usual, Mama wasn't holding nothin' back. Every year, we strip beds and wash curtains. We do windows and floors, and we even vacuum under stuff. We dust everything. Mama is real particular about how the house is for family comin'.

We have dinner at our house, mostly because Mama cooks better than anybody else. But we also do it because we live so close to town. Like I said, Tommy plows our road, so it is easier for folks to get to our place.

Mama has a big family. There's Aunt Lily and

her second husband, Uncle Bob. Her first husband was Mama's brother, Will, and even though he died, Aunt Lily is still family. She's the mama to three of my cousins. Uncle Thomas is Mama's other brother; he drinks a lot, but he's mighty funny. He's married to my Aunt Aggie, but she don't come anymore. She says she ain't goin' nowhere with the drunken fool. Mama doesn't like her much anyway, so it's all right. His two sons come and hang out with Tommy. Mama's sister, Aunt Rosie, comes too; her husband died in 1968, and ever since then, she thinks she can see the future. Mama says she is being ridiculous.

"Been waitin' to meet a man whose name starts with an 'S.' She could have been married four times now, but she keeps turning 'em down." Then she just shakes her head. "Fool of a woman!"

Still, Mama loves Rosie, and they are close friends.

Even Rosie has kids. There are four of 'em, and we have a good time. They all come, and us kids play hide-and-seek while the adults sit around watchin' football and talkin' about everything that happened over the year.

This year was a special one, as Daddy's cousin was comin' too. She's a hippy, Mama says. I'm not really sure what that all means, but Mama says it like it annoys her some.

"That girl just never grew up. She can't stay a hippie forever!"

I was too young to remember meeting her, so I was excited to see her. Her name was Jilly, and she was bringin' her friend, Burns, and his son. I just knew it was gonna be fun. She was from Alabama.

See, Daddy, he lived in Alabama when he was young, and he worked at the boat docks after graduation. It was Randall Pratt who brought him to Iowa and got him a job at the plastics factory. He has worked at Plastico for twenty years now.

He was only gonna work there for two years while he went to the community college. He met Mama, and they was gonna move to the city about sixty miles from here and start their own business. Daddy loves music, and he was gonna open a music store. They were gonna have books, too. Writers were gonna come and sign books. Poets could go there, too. They would read their poems and play their guitars while people watched and drank herbal tea.

But, from what I understand, Mama's brother, Will, got real sick. He had something wrong in his legs, and he couldn't help my grandfather anymore. So Daddy took over helpin' Pa around his farm after work, and he never moved to the city. Mama started watchin' my little cousins so Aunt Lily could get a job.

Uncle Will ended up goin' to the nursin' home where he died shortly after. Aunt Lily remarried right after that. Her and Uncle Bob moved away to Oregon, started a whole new bunch of cousins, and only come back at the holidays.

Daddy offered to move in with Pa and Memaw to help on the farm, but Memaw wouldn't hear of it.

"Suzanna, that Jack of yours don't have a farmin' bone in his body!" Memaw told her.

Soon after, she hired a farmhand from Baker's Flatt to come out three times a week. They got practically the whole family workin' out there now. The farmhand had three sons over the years, and they all pitch in and help Pa. They are all like family to us now. Even them sons got kids and wives now.

Since Mama and Daddy had decided against the city and didn't need to worry about Pa and the farm, they bought our big old house right here. Even though we don't farm, our house is a giant farmhouse. The Pratt family lived here for three generations before they built their new house on the other side of the creek. Daddy said he got this house real cheap 'cause he didn't want the land. There's nothin' real special about it 'cept it's big. There are two staircases. One is inside the front door, and the other is in the kitchen.

We don't use the one in the kitchen 'cept for storin' things. Why, there are boots and hats, some of Tommy's fishin' stuff, an old fan that don't work, some egg cartons Mama swears she will use someday, and a bunch of tin cans of every shape and size. Daddy says they are good for storin' things in. It's funny though. He just stores the cans. I don't think he has ever used one, and there must be thirty or more in there.

Downstairs is a livin' room, dinin' room, kitchen, bathroom, and Mama and Daddy's room. Upstairs is another bathroom and four bedrooms. Tommy, Becky, and I have our own rooms, and Jimmy and Emmy share.

There's an attic, too, and that is my favorite place

to hide. I always sneak up there sometime before Thanksgiving and set up my hidin' spot.

While Becky and Mama were gettin' out the good dishes, I went up to the attic. The stairs up to the attic are just outside the bathroom, and we keep some extra supplies on them. I maneuvered around bottles of shampoo and packages of Ivory soap. I noticed Mama had bought some new towels, and they were there too.

Once in the attic, I noticed Mama had been cleanin' out some old boxes of clothes. I saw some of the outfits I had outgrown last summer. Emmy's winter coat from the year before was there too. It was lyin' on an old trunk. Arrangin' boxes of holiday decorations, I made a nice little hole to crawl into where I wouldn't be found. I camouflaged the openin' with the clothes Mama had sorted through.

I threw Emmy's coat on top of the clothes heap. It was perfect. I sat down by the old trunk to make sure even the smallest child couldn't see me. It was still perfect. While I sat there, I thought about my cousins and how I hadn't seen some of them in so long. I thought of Jilly and tried to remember her. I almost thought I could. And I thought of her friend, Burns, and his son, both of whom I had never met. I was excited for them to come.

As I started to get up from the floor, my shirt caught on the latch of the old trunk. As I unhooked my shirt, I was grateful it didn't rip. Mama tends to get mad at us for things like that. But the latch on that old trunk popped, and the lid eased open just a bit. As I tried to close it, it kept poppin' back open. I opened the top to move what was stoppin' it from closin'.

Inside that trunk was the most amazin' sight. It was full of books. Beautiful, leather bound books of all shapes and sizes were scattered about. I picked up the top book. It was the most beautiful book I had ever seen. It was dark brown leather with golden flecks all over it.

The cover was dusty, and I could feel the grit on my fingers. The page edges were yellowed from age, and they too were gritty with dust. I started to open it when a card fell to the floor. There was a bouquet of wildflowers on the front. They were beautiful flowers like the ones along side our house. Inside the card was the most beautiful writin' I had ever seen. It was small and flowed together perfectly. It was just like the samples in the school books, only it was fancier. It was somewhat faded, but what it said was simple.

My love for you, Jonas, has grown since the birth of our beautiful daughter. Your loving wife,

Eliza

I stared at the card for just a minute. Then I opened the book. There was an inscription. It, too, was beautifully penned. The writing was just as perfect, but harder to make out, as it was very faded. It said:

Dearest Eliza,
With your light eyes and my light hair, our daughter is beau-
tiful. She and you are the light of my life.

Yours forever.
Jonas

At the bottom was the date, September 10, '62. That was my birthday. It was written about me. But my parents weren't named Jonas and Eliza. My parents were Jack and Suzie.

At that moment, it occurred to me that I didn't look like my parents or my sisters. I didn't resemble anyone in my family. I had light hair and light eyes, and everyone else had dark hair and, like Daddy always said, "chestnut eyes like Mama."

But he never talked about me like that. I came to them by accident … serendipity! I felt a shiver. I stuck the book under my shirt.

Color had never mattered to me 'til then. Smell had never mattered 'til then. Suddenly I could smell the musty old attic, and it felt cold and dark. All of a sudden, everything and nothin' mattered all at the same time. Right then, for the first time, I knew I was adopted.

CHAPTER THREE

I never knew anybody that was adopted, so I didn't have a clue how it all worked. I didn't cry, and I wasn't mad. I thought about Mama and Daddy. I thought how different we were, but how we were also the same. Daddy loved books, and so did I. But I guess I could have just got that from bein' around him. I liked music, and I even played the clarinet. Daddy played the guitar and liked to sing. But again, I guess I could have got that from bein' around him.

Mama was real pretty, like a movie star. She had dark hair and dark eyes, and she was tall like a model. I was short and had light eyes. People always used to say, "Where'd you get those peepers, Sippy Johnson?"

Or sometimes they would say, "Them are some shinin' lights."

I never thought much about it, and I always kind of liked the attention. Not so much anymore. Now, it just made me feel different.

I didn't have a notion what to do next. I tried to think of movies I had seen about this stuff, and I couldn't think of one. As I left the attic, I tried to think of what Becky would do.

She would march right up to Mama and Daddy and demand an explanation. She would holler and cry and flip her hair all around. I just couldn't do that. As I got to my room, I thought about it again. Nope, I just couldn't do that.

I entered my room and all I could do was start pacin'. I went back and forth. Back and forth. I started thinkin' about what led me to find the book. After all these years of hidin' in the attic and playin' around Mama and Daddy's old things, I had never found it before. Then I remembered my shirt gettin' caught. Was this a sign? Was I supposed to find this? Why? Why now? I looked up at my ceilin'. I knew we needed to talk.

"Why?" I asked.

"Why?" I asked again.

I asked over and over, but I got nothin'. I told Him I didn't understand. He needed to be a little more clear with his signs. I still got nothin'. I took the book I had found and slid it under the mattress of my bed. I put it in between the mattress and the box spring. It would be safe there.

I planned to read the book later, but I knew I'd better join Mama and Becky before they came lookin' for me. I suddenly didn't care about Thanksgiving or my cousins. I didn't want any hide-and-seek or family time. I didn't want anything.

Downstairs, Mama and Becky had all the dishes pulled and washed. The linens were out and nicely arranged to cover the tables. The extra chairs from the garage had been brought in, and Emmy and Jimmy were busy wipin' them off. Daddy was in the basement. No doubt he was workin' on another project to show the family. Tommy had been given the job of cleanin' out the back porch, since it was mostly his stuff anyway. Mama and Becky were at the table havin' a cup of tea and wrappin' silverware in pretty napkins.

I sat down to join them, and Mama scooted some silverware my way as she thanked me for coming back.

"Don't know where you are always runnin' off to, but we appreciate your return." I didn't have to answer, as she went on. "Have you met this boy your sister knows?"

Becky must have been talkin' about that Aaron boy again. I shook my head no as I told her, "Saw him goin' to gym when I was leavin' the library." And that is when I lied. For the first time in my life, I lied to my mama. "Miss Allen has given us an assignment about family. It's about findin' out where our families come from like the Pilgrims."

I was quite impressed with how fast I thought of it. I didn't cook it up; it just came out like the truth.

"We have to do research and stuff to find out all about our ancestors." I figured Mama would get all nervous and stuff, but she didn't. Not at all. In fact, she did the opposite.

"That sounds fun. When Jilly comes, she could probably help. She knows all those stories and legends about all the great-great-grandparents."

By this time, my lie had become like second nature. "Well, I need to know everything. I need birthdays and anniversaries and everybody's brothers and sisters. I have to know your Mama's and Daddy's birthdays even," I continued with still no response.

She was excited about it. I didn't get it. Wouldn't she be afraid I would find out the truth?

"I even wanna talk with Memaw and Pa about stuff they remember too. I want to know things about you and Daddy when you were younger. And about when I was born."

That did it. All of a sudden, Mama got real nervous. She said her and Daddy were nothin' special. She got up from the table real fast and put her cup in the sink. She started fidgetin' with stuff that was already done. Even Becky noticed, and she made a funny face.

"Oh, Mama. It sounds interestin' to learn about you and Daddy." Becky smiled and continued, "And about when we were born."

I realized I had upset Mama, and I felt bad about it. I quickly changed the subject to Alabama and Jilly. That really fired Mama up.

"Combin' the country like gypsies." She got serious. "One time when that boy of his—Joey is his name—why, he was just a little boy, and they went into Mexico. I guess you can walk in from somewhere in Texas. They just walked into Mexico, and then they went to walk back across. But they had no identification for Joey! They almost had to stay there! Took 'em a few hours, I guess, to convince the Mexican government to let them come back." She continued wipin' clean counters as she talked. "Thought they would have learned their lesson then and stopped all their gallivantin', but they haven't."

They travel a lot. They have been to Colorado, New York City, and even the ocean in California. They have spent years always travelin'. Burns's little boy has never been to school or nothin'. Jilly teaches him herself right in their motor home. I can't imagine him knowin' much if he ain't never had a teacher. He was comin' too, and I was more excited than ever to meet him.

Then I remembered he wasn't any real relation to me. None of them were.

Becky was back to talkin', and I figured I had better pay attention or she would be buggin' me to tell her what was wrong. She was talkin' about the assignment from Miss Allen again, and Mama was gettin' tired of hearin' it.

One thing about Becky is that she is a talker. She can talk for about three minutes and not even take a breath. Daddy used to tell us to hold onto the table when Becky started tellin' a story at supper. Sometimes she talks so fast all the words run together, and it's like a foreign language. Sometimes it is hard to shut her up.

But I knew how to stop Becky from talkin' about this subject. I just asked her about Aaron. And, yep, that did it. Soon she was describin' his eyes and his hair and something about the way he looked at her in social studies when she knew where Persia was. It was dumb.

I finished silverware wrappin' without further

incident, but I couldn't focus on foldin' the napkins. Mama insists everything be so perfect. I don't understand that at all. We are just gonna undo them and slop all our missed attempts at eatin' all over them. I never have figured why Mama never opened her own restaurant. She could have been great at that.

She can cook anything, and some stuff she cooks, she just makes up as she goes. It makes her real mad when she can't remember how she made somethin'. Especially if we really like it. We figured out a long time ago to ask Mama what it is before we eat. If she doesn't have a name for it, we best not make it a favorite 'cause that means she don't have a clue how to make it again.

Mama was busy lookin' through the cookbook at desserts. She said she wanted somethin' different this year. Somethin' special is what she said. Becky was in "la la land" talking about Aaron so finished foldin' the napkins without noticing I didn't help. Emmy was done with the chairs and was now colorin' in the living room. Jimmy was mad at her and lookin' through his baseball cards. Tommy was done with the porch, and he ran down to talk to Daddy about a huntin' trip the Pratt boys were plannin'. Guess the weather changed it from fishin' to huntin'. Sometimes, boys really confuse me.

Daddy wasn't much into the huntin' thing. He didn't mind fishin' and would even fry up some fish now and then, but he didn't hunt. He didn't stop Tommy from doin' it, but he didn't want details, and he didn't want to eat anything Tommy killed. That was just a rule.

The Pratts own a cabin up in Falls Hollow, and they were goin' there to stay overnight. Daddy was funny about us kids stayin' overnight at places. He said he didn't sleep good if he didn't know we were tucked in. Last summer, when Laura Wilkins had a slumber party, I had to call him right before I went to sleep so he knew I was safe and sound. It was embarrassin' to do at the party, but afterwards all the girls said how neat that was. I never did tell him I woke up with peanut butter in between my toes and my next-day underpants in the freezer. He probably wouldn't have liked that.

Mama was excited about the recipe for Lemon Truffles she found so I asked to go to town and check out books at the library. She said I could, but Tommy had to give me a ride. I didn't mind that so much, except he gave me a time limit on when he would pick me up. I only had one hour.

I wasn't sure what I was lookin' for, but knew I had to look for somethin'. I started in the adoption books. I looked at books on how to and when to. I looked at books on why and why not. The librarian, Mrs. Wilkins, kept looking at me as if I was gonna steal somethin'. I figured she probably knew the truth and was shocked that I did. I was hopin' she would say somethin' so I could play along, but she didn't. She just kept watchin' me.

I looked at books on heredity and family history. I didn't understand much of those. There were lots of big words, and while I am not dumb, I did just turn eleven. I was still lookin' when I saw Tommy come inside and stand by the front door. I hid behind the shelves 'til I could get the books I wanted to take home. He saw me and motioned for me to hurry. I checked out three books that day, and they were all about adoption.

Tommy was talkative on the way home. I guess Daddy told him he could go to the cabin with the Pratts. They wouldn't be goin' 'til after Christmas, so Daddy managed to get a promise of some extra chores in exchange.

He was older than all of us and could have left home a while ago, but he stayed in school at the college outside of town and had a part-time job at Montgomery Ward in the car department. Mama always wanted him to go to art school, but he didn't. He was real good at drawin' stuff, and he probably could have gotten a job doin' it, but he didn't think so. Besides, he would rather tear apart a car and put it back together, and Daddy said that was good talent, too.

Tommy's always workin' on cars and tractors for people around town. One time he worked all summer for Mr. Baker's nephew. He saved all the money and bought his own truck. Then last winter, he and Mr. Baker did some tradin', and he got the scoop thing to attach to the front. Mr. Baker got the best deal outta that, though, 'cause now he gets his lane scooped for free.

The church called the other day and paid Tommy

to scoop their parkin' lot, and the preacher asked God to bless him in church. So now a bunch of people have started callin' for him. I guess Tommy is startin' to get good out of it, too.

I am pretty sure he is crushin' on the preacher's daughter. He sure does smile a lot when she's around. She works up at the corner store, and Tommy spends a lot of time there. He always comes home whistlin' and smilin'.

We stopped in there on the way home from the library. She was workin', and Tommy was whistlin'.

"That is just sweet of ya. Pickin' Sippy up from the library," she said as she smiled real sweet. I am pretty sure she likes Tommy, too.

"Can't have her walkin' home in the cold, now can I?" he told her and put his arm around my shoulders. I didn't say nothin' about Mama sayin' he had to, and I tried not to flinch when he touched me all sweet. I was sure I could use it as blackmail later.

She was real pretty. I could see why Tommy would like her.

"It was nice of you to do the church plowin', too. We all prayed that you would be blessed big for doin' that," she said. Tommy mumbled something I missed.

"Hope we see you in church sometime." She smiled.

With that, I figured he would run outta that store and all the way home, but he didn't.

"Maybe you will," he said.

My eyeballs probably got as big as gumballs. I never heard Tommy say nothin' of the sort. When

Memaw makes us say grace at her house, he usually makes noises and tries to get us little kids to giggle. He never likes talkin' about God with her. I like hearin' Bible stories, but not Tommy.

Maybe you will. I couldn't get it outta my head. I just stood there waiting to see what happened next. It was like watchin' a movie on the television. Then she rattled on about youth group and get-togethers and guitars. She said something about a novella her mama wrote and something about a play. She was real excited and talked real fast like Becky. I missed a lot of it, but not Tommy.

He got every single word. He admitted to not being able to sing a note or play any instruments, which I was glad for. I would have hated to have to teach him the clarinet. But then the real shock came.

"I'm pretty good at art. If ya need a stagehand to help paint the set, let me know," he said.

I couldn't believe it. He never told anybody about his art. He would get so mad at Mama when she told people.

Well, you can imagine Sarah's smile then.

"Oh, that would be great. The play's not 'til spring, but we've been meetin' on Tuesdays at three and on Wednesdays just before church services," she said. "We want to be prepared, and we would love you to join us."

Tommy took it all in. I could tell he was really concentratin'. I was gonna remember the dates in case he forgot, but I knew Sarah wouldn't let him forget.

He would be back, and she was not gonna let him off the hook now. I could tell.

I could tell she liked him too. Suddenly some of the stuff Becky told me was startin' to make sense. I was startin' to get it. That was kinda scary. But it was sweet how Tommy talked to her. The way he looked at her reminded me of the way Daddy looks at Mama. I never realized how handsome Tommy was 'til right that moment.

We finally had to go 'cause there were other customers. Tommy whistled all the way home. There must be somethin' to that whistlin'. It didn't take us long to get there. He didn't say much to me, but he did ask me what a novella was. It was cute and funny and made me laugh. We walked in the back door just in time to hear Mama's news.

Memaw had a heart attack, and Thanksgiving dinner was cancelled.

CHAPTER FOUR

MAMA and Daddy took off fast to go to the hospital. Me and Becky got the little ones tucked into bed. Becky was frantic. She didn't know what to do after Emmy and Jimmy were in bed. She kept talkin' about Memaw and tellin' old stories and such. I felt like I had little people inside my body tryin' to get out. It felt as if they were bangin' on the walls of my chest and scrapin' at my stomach to free themselves.

Tommy had left to go back up to the store. He said he would be right back, but I knew he wouldn't. I understood. Becky didn't, and she was darn mad about it. I finally had to tell her I thought Tommy had a crush on Sarah Jameson. That didn't help Becky none. She was still raisin' cane about him being gone.

I told her I didn't want to talk about Memaw anymore. I didn't like telling old stories. It made me feel like she wasn't gonna be back, and in my heart, I knew she would. I went up to my room, and that is when I had my second real talk with God.

"Hi, it's me," I said while lookin' up at my ceilin'. "I know you are there and listenin', and I just wanna tell ya that I ain't ready to give her to you yet. I'm sure you think she is swell and would make a fine addition to your Heaven and all, but you can't have her! Not yet.

"I'm only eleven, and I've got quite a few years of learnin' left, and she is a real good teacher. Think about it awhile. She taught me about You. She taught me to crochet and how to sew on a button.

"She taught Becky how to make sweet tea the right way, and I heard Mama say just the other day she was gonna do a cookbook for the church fundraiser this summer. And that money is gonna help send teenagers to missionary camp! So it's not just me, it's everybody!

"So you can't have her! You just go find someone else until we are done with her. I'll let you know when that is, OK?

"Thank you." I nodded as if to excuse myself.

I sat there just a minute and tried to make sense of it all. I didn't like soundin' all stern as if I was tellin' Him what to do, but I was darn upset. It must have been OK with Him, though, 'cause lightnin' didn't strike. There wasn't a big, scary voice or anything.

I thought of the previous few weeks. I didn't understand. I went back in my mind through each and every day, and I couldn't come up with one sign that would explain it to me. I thought about the day before, and I still didn't get it. I ended up fallin' asleep that night and woke up about four in the mornin'.

Mama and Daddy were back, and I could hear Daddy playin' his guitar. I wasn't sure if that was good or bad, but I went downstairs anyway.

They were both sittin' in the livin' room. Mama

had her nightclothes on, and her hair was combed down out of her usual ponytail. They heard me comin' down the stairs, and they was lookin' right at me when I come around the corner. The looks on their faces wasn't sad, so I knew Memaw was OK.

"Don't you worry, Sippy," Mama said. "Things are fine. We will talk in the mornin'. Now get on up to bed."

I kissed and hugged each of them, got a glass of milk, and did what I was told. I fell asleep to Daddy's distant music.

The next day we got the only explanation needed. Memaw was fine, but she needed lots of rest and special medicine. Thanksgiving dinner remained cancelled. Now if ya ask me, I thought that was dumb. Ain't Thanksgiving a celebration? Ain't it a time for being thankful?

Well, I was sure thankful Memaw was OK, and I couldn't think of a better reason to celebrate, but Mama didn't think so. She said she needed to be takin' care of her and didn't have time to be entertainin'. I didn't get that at all, but that was how it was, and we all just took turns visitin' her. I was disappointed about Thanksgiving, though.

Memaw stayed in the hospital for a couple days, and the day before Thanksgiving she went home. Mama spent a lot of time there, and Becky went with her. Tommy was busy with Sarah and the church play. Daddy was doing his regular thing in the basement, and Emmy and Jimmy were bein' nine and seven.

This left me doing my own thing, which was a whole lot of nothin'.

I had my books from the library, though. Max had come over, so we started readin' about adoption.

"Listen, Max. Most adoption decisions come from the parents being young," I read from the book.

"My parents were probably young," I said as I made a mental note to get a book about that next time.

"What's another reason?" Max asked.

"Poor," I repeated what I had read. "My parents were probably poor,"

I was gettin' sad. Reading about all of that wasn't makin' me feel any better. In fact it was making me feel worse. Max knew me real good, so he knew I wasn't likin' it none.

"We should do this some other time, Sippy. And don't feel too bad. Remember that puppy we found a couple years ago? And we had to give him away. When my pa told us that puppy needed more room to be happy and all, we worked real hard to find him a good home. 'Cause we wanted him to be happy. Ya remember that, right?" I did remember. I nodded. "Maybe your folks thought that about you too."

Max and me was best friends. I don't remember first meetin' him. It's as if he's always been there. It sounds strange to say that, but it's true. Our folks bowled together when we were little, and Mama said we just took to each other right off. Then when we started kindergarten, we was already friends.

I asked him once when we were down by the creek if it was weird bein' friends with a girl.

"No. It's not like you're a real girl. You're Sippy. It's different."

"I am too a real girl!" I exclaimed, standin' up with my hands on my hips.

"You know what I mean. Now, you gonna fish or what? 'Cause you got a bite!"

I almost fell in the creek that day trying to grab my pole. We laughed about that most of the afternoon, but I never asked him again if it was weird. And he never mentioned it either.

"So, ya think my folks wanted me to be happy?" I finally asked about what he had said.

"Yeah, I do. That is what I think."

"I am, ya know," I told him, "but I still want to know why."

"I know, Sippy." He gathered up his coat. "I gotta get home. Ma wants me to clean the garage."

I walked him downstairs, and he let himself out without sayin' good-bye. He did that a lot. He told me once he felt like sayin' good-bye meant you would never see each other again.

"I think it's 'cause my grandpa said good-bye to me, and then he died."

"But Max, not everyone will die if you say good-bye."

"I know, but it's just a thing for me. So I never say it."

And so he never did.

I decided to make a snack, and I watched television

for awhile. When I took my dishes to the kitchen, I heard honkin'. It was loud and repeated honkin'. I looked out of the window above the sink. I could see the motor home pullin' into our driveway.

It was Jilly and Burns! I ran out the back door after yellin' into the basement to Daddy. As I got outside they were getting' out and stretchin'. They were in Minnesota when they heard about Memaw. But, since Iowa was on their way home to Alabama, they came to see us anyway. I had forgotten they were comin'.

Daddy's cousin Jilly was beautiful. She didn't look her age at all, which was over forty, if I remember right. She had light hair that was very long. It was so long it was almost to the waist of her jeans. She pulled it out of her eyes in the front and held it back with one small barrette. She was real tan and had the biggest smile I had ever seen. She wore lots of neck-laces and bracelets and had a ring on nearly every finger.

Her T-shirt was white with writin' on the front. I couldn't tell what it said 'cause she was bendin' every which way, and her coat kept fallin' in front of the words. Her friend, Burns, had hair just as long as hers, but he pulled it back into a ponytail. He was tan too, and he looked older than Jilly. He had half of a beard and a tattoo of a snake on his arm.

He was wearin' jeans, and his T-shirt was plain black with long sleeves, which he'd pushed up to his elbows. He had a coat on, but it didn't have any sleeves. It was funny. I figured he was freezin'. I didn't see his son, Joey, at first, and I almost thought he didn't come when Jilly hollered at him to come on and say hi. I could see why Mama would get annoyed with them. They didn't act like adults at all.

They had the music in the motor home louder than I had ever heard Becky's. Mama called it a motor home, but it looked like a bus to me. Jilly called it a bus. There were beads hangin' in the windows, and a big peace sign covered a tire hangin' on the back. I just stood there and waited for them to see me. Jilly finished her stretchin' and stood by the door of their home on wheels.

She motioned for Joey to come with her, and surprisingly, he looked like a normal kid. He was older than me, but he looked just like any boy in my school. I expected his hair to be draggin' on the ground and his clothes to be worn and tattered. But they weren't. He looked normal. I was glad but shocked at the same time.

Jilly and Joey walked to the front of the bus and joined Burns, who waved but didn't smile. I waved back but didn't move from my perch up on our porch. Daddy came out the back door, and then, like Daddy does, he just welcomed them.

"How was your trip?" He hugged Jilly first. "Lookin' good, Jil," he added and shook Burns's hand.

"Ah, Ma's fine. Suzie is over there gettin' her settled in for the day. She'll be back soon." He motioned up to where I was. Daddy talked with his hands a lot. Mama told us that when they was first married, Daddy went to an auction uptown.

"Came home with 140 boxes of florescent

lightbulbs. No fixtures, of course. Just the lightbulbs. He isn't allowed at auctions anymore!"

As I stood there, Jilly looked up.

"Hi," I said quietly.

I got the full effect of Jilly then. She beamed with excitement, and in her very thick Alabama twang she said, "Well now. Serendipitay! You get on down here-a and give me a hug-a!" She didn't breathe. "You know ya'll gotta give a hug to your familay!"

Her accent was thick. There could be no mistake. She lived in the south. I did what she said.

And boy could she hug. I never had been hugged like that in my entire life. It was firm and soft all at once. And it was warm. I liked it a lot. I liked her. She was so excited to see me, and she kept talkin' about how big I was and how pretty I was. She just kept pointin'.

"Burns, look! See, Burns? Do ya see it?" She wasn't waiting for answers, and he wasn't intendin' on givin' them. He half-smiled, I think.

I was not used to so much attention. I kind of liked it, but at the same time, it felt odd. We went on inside, and I got them some of Becky's sweet tea and some cookies that Mama had made. I sat at the table while they talked to Daddy about their adventures.

Daddy was so interested in everyplace they had ever been. He listened to story after story and never got bored. They told us they were headin' back to Alabama after our house. They were gonna stay in Alabama for six months. That was new for them.

Jilly had spent her whole life travelin' the country.

She usually stayed in one place for only a few weeks. She met Burns about ten years ago, and now they both had people all across the country that would put 'em up or give 'em work for a while if they needed it. Her "road friends," as she called 'em, were her family, too, and she said if any of them needed help, she would be there. It sounded like a gypsy life to me, just like Mama said.

Joey was quiet. I expected that after never bein' to school and all. I felt sorry for him. Daddy asked me if I could show him around outside. I cringed at the thought at first, but then I thought maybe I could teach him somethin'. Boy was I wrong!

We grabbed our coats, although his was barely a jacket by definition. We left out the back door while they talked about Minnesota. Joey and I tried small talk, but I am not very good at that. He told me they left two weeks earlier from New York. Jilly had some friends in Minnesota, and they had stopped there for a few days.

Joey said they had a boy around his age who played a guitar real good, so it was pretty fun. I had never heard of the place or the people, so I just smiled and tried not to be rude.

I took him around back and showed him the little mini-creek. I told him about Dyers Creek and how it flows into the Mississippi. I told him you can float all the way there from our front door. He told me about a river in Arizona. I showed him Johnson Mountain. He told me there were mountains in Colorado that have tunnels drilled in them, and the road goes right through them. Those would be real mountains.

He was really smart and told me a lot of stuff, but we were freezin', so we went on inside. Mama had called and was on her way. Daddy had put on some soup that Mama had made earlier in the day. She had taken all the fixings that would have been Thanksgiving dinner and put it in a big pot. It seemed like a waste of good food to just throw it all together, but Mama had a way with food, and it smelled great.

Daddy told me I would be roomin' with Becky that night so they could have my room. I didn't like that at all, but I agreed and smiled like it didn't bother me. Jilly burst in, "I will have no such thang!" She looked at me. "Don't you worry, Serendipitay, we will sleep in our bus."

I really liked her.

Mama and Becky got home before the soup was hot, and Tommy pulled in right behind them. They did the formal huggin' and "how ya been," and we all sat down to soup. Becky heated up some rolls, and Daddy talked Mama into eating some of the pie she had made. I was glad Jilly still came.

We talked about Memaw and how good she was doin'. We talked about school and how it was for all of us. I felt bad talkin' about that as Joey couldn't talk about his school. But he did join in when we talked about Tommy's hunting trip coming up. Joey learned about trappin' from their Indian friend, Cloud.

"He taught me how to catch trout with my bare hands, too," he told us. "The water is so clear, and they will swim right by your legs while you're wading in the streams. And if you are fast enough, you reach in and grab them.

"I caught one once that was as big as my size nine shoes. Put it in my pouch to take back to camp. Of course, I kept opening it to check on it. And sure enough, it jumped right back into the stream."

He was very good at tellin' stories.

No one at his camp believed he caught one so big, but I did. I just knew he would have no reason to lie about it. I liked Joey, and I was glad he wasn't as dumb as I thought he would be. He's actually seen some of the things I have only read about such as the Grand Canyon, Niagara Falls, Yosemite National Park, the Alamo, and the Statue of Liberty. I was impressed, and so was Tommy.

Tommy talked about his trips with the Pratts, Charlotte's Cove, and Camp Willow Tree. Joey said he thought they would be neat places to see. Tommy even told them about the sets he was creating for the church play. I didn't know what had gotten into Tommy. But it was real cute.

Mama was so happy, although you could tell she was confused. Becky let it slip that it was all about a girl, and we all laughed. Even Tommy. It was a great supper, and we were all enjoyin' talkin' and laughin'. It made us not worry so much about Memaw. It made Mama not worry so much.

Jilly talked about Alabama and all the family that had moved away from down there. She said just her and some distant cousins were left. I liked hearin' all the stories, and I was thrilled to hear about family until I remembered they were not my real family. I had almost forgotten. I suddenly became sad when I realized I was not even related to Jilly.

I really liked her, and we had a lot in common. I actually realized at that moment that I kind of looked like her. Our eyes were light. Our hair was blonde. She was short like me. She liked to read. She liked music and had played the flute back in high school. She always wanted to learn piano but never did.

Mama and Daddy had me take clarinet because we didn't have room for a piano, and the music teacher said clarinet was a lot like the piano. I never did see that connection. But I did see one to Jilly.

I felt very connected to Jilly. As I sat there and listened, I watched her talk. I felt like I knew her. I wanted to know her better. I felt so relaxed with her. She was funny, and she smiled a lot. I really liked that about her.

Burns was quiet, but like Joey, when he did say somethin', it was always somethin' no one else knew. Jilly talked about everything and nothin'. She just talked all the time. We had sat there listenin' to Jilly's stories for most of the evenin' before I said much of anything.

When I did finally speak, I have no idea where the words came from. I didn't plan any of what came out of my mouth that night. It was like someone else was talkin' for me.

"I'm goin' with you." I looked right at Jilly. I didn't ask. I didn't hint. I just said outright that I was going with them when they went. Daddy laughed at first, and Mama was silent; she knew I was serious. Then Daddy realized it too.

"Oh, you can't miss school." Daddy spoke first.

"Maybe next time," Mama said.

Jilly was lookin' right into my eyes. She didn't say a word. She hadn't been quiet the whole time 'til then, and she was speechless. Burns, too, was silent. He just looked at Jilly. Joey spoke up for the first time in awhile with excitement.

"Oh, that would be so cool." But he soon fell silent as he looked around the table. Jilly continued to just look at me.

Mama and Daddy were still comin' up with reasons against the idea. Burns had finally opened up. He agreed with Mama and Daddy's arguments but had none of his own. Jilly still had not said a word. She just watched me as I went back and forth between her and Mama and her and Daddy.

She never faltered. That I could tell. She just watched me. Finally she sighed. It was as if that sigh was stuck in her, and lettin' it out allowed her to speak. But there wasn't one person prepared for what she said. Not even me.

"Why I think that is a fabulous idea, and I would like nothin' more than to take you with us, Serendipi-tay, and get to know you better!"

The whole room fell silent. Becky stopped mid-sentence. Tommy's smile left his face. Emmy and Jimmy started paying attention, and Mama and

Daddy just stared at her. Burns looked down at his hands, and Joey just looked at Mama and Daddy.

I looked back, and Jilly was still looking right at me. I could not look away from her then. I remember just sittin' there with her eyes melted into mine. We were like one. It was like there was no one else in the room. My heart was beatin' so loud I was sure everybody could hear it.

I felt a tear trickle out of my eye and run down my cheek. I'm not sure what was goin' on in my mind then. I just knew, like I knew my name, that I felt closer to Jilly than anyone ever. I felt a strong yearnin' in me. And I was sure, absolutely sure, I had to go with her.

And there was one more thing I was sure of. Jilly knew who my parents were.

CHAPTER FIVE

THAT little conversation at the table that night ended just as abruptly as it started, and I'm not quite sure who ended it. I know Mama fidgeted a bit before Daddy had her make some coffee. Tommy and Becky tried unsuccessfully to change the subject.

"How 'bout them White Sox? You watch any baseball, there, Burns?" Tommy wasn't much into sports really, so it sounded odd. Becky smacked him in the shoulder. Of course, she thought she could do better.

"Baseball isn't in season now. It's football that's on now. Probably a Vikings fan, right?" Daddy and Tommy both looked at her. "Well, he kinda looks like the guy on their hats. The beard thing. And the hair … "

Becky stopped talkin'. She put her hands down as she was pointin' to Burns's face and touchin' her own to further her point. She looked down at her lap and then frantically around the room for somethin' to do.

"I'm gonna get the little ones ready for bed now," Becky said as she stood. Jimmy and Emmy protested together.

"No, we don't wanna go to bed." Mama must have shot them a look 'cause they stopped their argument and immediately went with Becky. Burns looked at Joey, and without a word from either, Joey went outside to their bus. Jilly and I hadn't moved. We was both still sittin' there. We were listenin' to the talkin' but not participatin'. Mama brought coffee to the table.

"Jilly? Cream?" Mama offered.

"Suzie, I'm gonna make myself some tea if that's all right." Jilly got up from the table, and I watched her go.

"Hits the spot," Burns said as he sat his cup down. I noticed then that he did look like the man on the football helmets. Without the horns, of course.

"We can go into the livin' room. It's more comfortable in there."

Mama grabbed her cup. Daddy and Burns followed. I cleared the table of plates leftover from the pie we ate. Jilly had her tea and headed to the livin' room. She didn't say a word, but she kissed the top of my head as I walked past. I did the dishes and went up to bed.

Over the next few days, Mama spent a lot of time at the farm helpin' Pa with Memaw. She got stronger and stronger, and we all got to visit for a bit each day. Joey and I became great friends in a short time, and Jilly helped Becky around the house.

The Stevenson family, the ones Memaw hired years ago to help, don't work much in the winter. She says there ain't enough for them to do to be hangin' around. So they have a shop uptown that they open in the fall. They sell all kinds of seasonal stuff. Our big drugstore don't even have shovels or nothin'. Anything at all you need for winter is at Stevenson's. They start by havin' a big costume sale at Halloween.

We get our costumes there, and if we need one, we all get a new winter coat. Mama shops there for all her decoratin' stuff. People come all the way from Bakers Flatt for the Christmas stuff. Jilly and Burns went up and got them all winter coats. Burns got one with sleeves.

Burns helped Daddy, or he tried to anyway. I knew as good as anybody, Daddy was subjectin' him to some of his inventions. Burns would come upstairs for sweet tea scratchin' his head. Us kids all knew what he might be hearin' and seein', and we all understood. Jilly knew, too, but she would play along. She would ask Burns what was funny or what was wrong. He never could give her much of an answer, and sometimes he couldn't speak at all.

He would just look at her with this look. Bewildered is what Mama always called it in Daddy.

"Oh, Jack. Get that bewildered look off your face right this minute!" Mama would say. She always knew when Daddy had figured out somethin' he was thinkin' about. He would always plead with her after that to come downstairs and see. You know, thinkin' back, I don't think she ever did.

I never mentioned goin' to Alabama, and no one mentioned it to me. But I still wanted to go. I even thought I could sneak into their bus when they weren't lookin'. But I knew deep down Mama would be expectin' us kids to say our proper farewells, and I would be missed in the head count.

I spent a lot of time at the library. One day, while I looked for more books on adoption and teen pregnancy, it just made me feel sad. I decided to get some books on writing.

Miss Allen really had given us an assignment over our break, and I decided I should start doin' some of it. Although it wasn't about family like I told Mama, it was a writin' assignment, and, since I never have been much of a writer, I wanted to make sure my verbs were right. As I searched for grammar books, I wished it was about family.

While I was there I heard the librarian talkin' about someone who was gonna have a baby but was gonna put it up for adoption.

I felt a rush of sadness, but I also felt guilt for listenin' in. Mama had always said for us to mind our business. She said we shouldn't partake in gossipin', but I couldn't stop. She didn't see me standin' there. My face was hidden behind *The Elements of Style*.

I didn't catch any names, but Mrs. Wilkins was tellin' her friend about the girl.

" … sad that she is gettin' her support from a book instead of family in her time of need," Mrs. Wilkins told the woman.

"Well, she is doin' right by the child. Ain't no business of a young girl raisin' a baby. Why she is just a baby herself. I feel bad for her," her friend said. I felt bad too, and I wondered if my real mother had that kinda trouble.

Did she feel sad and alone when I was comin' along? I reckoned, if she didn't have a good family, she would have been scared, and that might have been why she gave me away. I wished there would have been someone close to her she could have talked to when she was troubled. I wished I had someone close I could go to.

I was startled suddenly by a too-familiar voice callin' me.

"Sweet thang!" Jilly was happy as ever. "We been wonderin' when ya'll be comin' on home. Ya'll get what ya needin' now?"

Jilly, with her smooth twang of a voice, had snuck right up behind me. I hoped she didn't see what I did. I hoped she didn't know I was listenin' in on a private conversation.

Mama would have tanned my butt for sure; though I can't remember one time when she actually did that. She sure did have a way of makin' us think she would, though. I don't know how she did that. It must be in that book all mamas read.

I smiled at Jilly and told her I had what I needed. I checked out three books on writin', including *The Elements of Style,* and I asked for an extra week on all of them. Mrs. Wilkins called me honey that day, and I remember now thinkin' how strange that was. I had been friends with her daughter since we were little kids, and she always just called me Sippy, like everybody else. Jilly and I left the library and stopped to pick up Mama on our way home.

"Your daddy asked me to pick up your mama, and

I just happened to think ya'll would like a ride home too." She didn't wait for me to respond. "Had to head up to that auto store and ask Tommy about our bus. We are gettin' it serviced before we go, and Burns had a question about spark plugs."

I realized I loved hearin' her talk. Her voice was raspy but still girly. And that accent. I just couldn't get enough. I'm not sure why Burns didn't go, but Jilly didn't seem to mind.

We got to the farm, and Pa was just pullin' in from the back field. Even in the winter time, he worked out in the back. Although Memaw said she wasn't sure what it was he did back there. I heard Tommy tell the Pratt boys once that Pa had a still in the pasture somewhere. They was gonna sneak out there one night and try to find it, but I busted in and told them Pa and Daddy would have their hides if they got caught doing any such thing. I don't think Tommy ever did go out there, but I wouldn't put it past the Pratt boys none.

Pa walked in with us and hollered to Mama that we were there. Her and Memaw were in the front room. They had made a nice little area for Memaw to relax, so she didn't have to be in bed all the time. I went on in to see her while Jilly helped herself to some of the pie Mama had brought from home.

"Get me some of that there pie, too," I heard Pa tell Jilly as I walked down the hall.

I slipped off my coat and sat in the chair beside Memaw. She had a big window next to her. She sat in her rockin' chair lookin' out. The bird feeder was right in the center of her view. Even though it was covered in snow and there weren't any birds in sight, it was still pretty to see.

A neighborin' farm was off in the distance, and it gave her something to watch. The scenery was like a postcard ya see at the truck stop up on the highway. I remember Memaw lookin' so pretty. She had real dark eyes like Mama, but they smiled.

Now don't get me wrong; my mama is pretty. She is as pretty as any movie star, but there is something about Memaw's eyes that I can't rightly explain. It's not a glitter, but it's kinda like that. It's like there's a light in them. But it's more than that. They turn upward like they smile, even when she isn't smiling herself. She held out her hand, and I took it.

Her hands were always so warm. It was like she had been holdin' them over a campfire. And they were so soft. It was like when you rub powder on a baby. They were soft like that.

"How ya feelin'?" I asked her.

"Much better. But I need to be gettin' up and doin' for myself."

"Not 'til the doctor says so."

"Oh, those doctors. They don't know everything. That Pa of yours is wreckin' the house." We both giggled then.

"How's school? Those little ones still fightin'?"

I answered the easy question. "Still fightin' as always."

"And Tommy? How is he gettin' along with Miss Sarah?" She winked, and I wondered how she knew since she hadn't been to church. I realized Mama had probably told her.

"I think he likes her a lot. He whistles all the time," I whispered as if Tommy were there and might have heard me.

She smiled and asked how I liked Joey and Burns, but she didn't wait for me to answer.

"And what about that Jilly? Silly Jilly." She shook her head, and I laughed at her name for her. I didn't need to answer. She asked about Daddy and shook her head.

"As long as he isn't blowin' up the house, he is all right." She patted my knee.

I don't think she meant to say that out loud. But she smiled. I knew she loved Daddy. She approved of him from the start. Mama and Daddy told us the story many times about Daddy workin' in the river yards down in Alabama. Jilly's brother, Ray, worked there too. And that's how Daddy met Randall Pratt. Randall had gone down there to work for the winter. In the spring, he told Daddy he should come up to Iowa and work.

"Friend of mine's got a pretty sister. I could introduce ya. And we could get jobs at the new plastics plant," he told him.

So Daddy, Randall, and Jilly's brother all came up to Iowa.

"On a freight!" Ray and Jilly's mama would say all mad-like.

"It was just the thought of us workin' on a barge,

I guess," Daddy said. "But it paid good, so we worked all summer."

"Now that fall, Ray went back to Alabama," Mama continued the story. "But your Daddy stayed with his friend, Randall. They joined his family in farmin'. He wasn't much of a farmer, mind ya. But he was a good worker. He even did some work for other farmers around here, includin' my daddy—your pa."

She always said that part so proud and would pause a second or two before she continued.

"Well not long after, the plant opened, and he got a job there. He just made Iowa his home. Ray brought Jilly up a lot, and he even brought his new girlfriend up to meet us all. Ray was so smitten with his new girl, and he eventually just stayed in Alabama, and Jilly joined the Red Cross. Her travelin' started then, I think. We wouldn't see her for months at a time." She always broke into a big ol' smile, and then she'd say just as proud as ever, "As for your Daddy, he married that pretty sister!"

And she would just smile. It was always one of my favorite stories.

Memaw asked about me then. "How you comin' along with your school project?"

I didn't know how she knew about that. I hadn't told anyone. I didn't bring my books in. Then I realized she meant the "family project." The one I told mama about. The one I lied about. I just looked at her, and although her eyes still smiled, they were serious.

"You know, Sippy. You won't get your answers

from books. Or people. You get your answers from inside you." She was still serious but kind. She smiled. "Have you looked inside you?"

She reached out, and she touched my chest right where my heart is. She didn't expect an answer, which I was glad for because I didn't have one. I just looked at her and waited. I knew there was more to hear.

"Find what is inside you. Nothing else matters." She motioned out toward the kitchen. "Now tell your mama to bring me a slice of that pie."

She kissed my hand, and I told her I loved her. She said she loved me more. I almost ran into Mama as I left the room. She had a piece of pie and was lickin' Cool Whip off her finger, and I smiled as I walked past her and down the hall.

Jilly was in the kitchen with a big piece of pie in front of her and one for me. Pa had the radio on the talk show he liked. It was some kind of flea market show. People would call in and trade things. He sat silently and wrote down phone numbers as the callers rattled them off.

"I need some chicken wire. I got some hay bales and tire irons for trade," the caller stated.

Jilly and I giggled under our breath. She made funny faces as she mocked Pa. I laughed as I envisioned him hauling home some spare bike parts, pickle jars, and rabbit cages.

Jilly turned the flame off the whistlin' tea kettle, and Pa grabbed it from the stove after he put his plate in the sink. He let the water run cold so he could use it to cool down his instant coffee. He sat with us.

There was a permanent stain on the table where he would lay his spoon. A few freckles of coffee always lie right next to it. Pa asked Jilly when they were headin' home, and she explained about the parts for the bus they were waitin' on. She said Tommy was getting them the next mornin' and that they were leavin' in the afternoon.

He told her to be careful and not to be such a stranger.

"And tell that Burns to cut his hair, settle down, and get a real job."

She laughed and said she would tell him. There was somethin' in her laugh, though, that told me she wouldn't tell him that.

They were all nice to Jilly even though she was Daddy's cousin. And when Pa heard they was comin', he said he had always liked Jilly. "She's just likable." I understood that now.

I realized I left my parka in the front room, and I went to get it. Mama was gettin' her coat on, and Memaw was talkin' soft, but I could still hear what she said. I didn't hear it all, but I heard the important part. And Mama saw me just as Memaw said, "Let her go, Suzie. You gotta let Sippy go with Jilly. She needs to go."

CHAPTER SIX

I'M not sure 'bout all the grown-up details and all, but Burns and Jilly didn't leave the next day or the day after that. Mama had convinced them to stay through Christmas and the New Year. She called the principal and Miss Allen and got them to put some of my work together. She told them Jilly would be teachin' me and sendin' my work back to them for gradin'.

The school wasn't too happy about none of it, but Mama said it was a family issue and none of their business. I heard Mama and Daddy say I could just go to school in the summer if I got behind. Jilly said she would take care of it.

Burns worked for Mr. Baker and his nephew. He even did some farmwork for the Pratts, too. Jilly helped with Memaw and worked on Saturdays at the beauty shop takin' appointments and makin' herbal tea.

Now, mind ya, not much was said to me at this time about the trip. Christmas came and went. Of course, we were festive and spirited and all, and it was a good time, but it just felt different somehow. After the first of the year, Mama started getting me ready.

She just took over everything and started washin'

all my things and packin' me the essentials. She took me to Bakers Flatt, and we exchanged some of my Christmas clothes that were too small. She took me over to the beauty shop and let me get my hair cut. I was shocked about that 'cause she liked my hair long. I just got it cut up to the shoulders. And it kinda flipped outward on the ends. It looked real pretty, I thought.

Becky had been real quiet for days. Daddy let her get her job at the Dairy Mart, and she was savin' her money to buy a car. I thought she would have been real happy. I wasn't sure exactly, but she seemed sad.

Tommy was busy with Sarah, but he did manage to talk to me a bit one afternoon.

"You be sure and stay outta trouble now," he said.

"I will. But I don't think Jilly will let me get into trouble." I was organizin' some books on my bed. "Mama would have her stoned if she did," I added and laughed.

Tommy laughed too.

"And don't turn into some kinda hippy." He handed me a bag of candy.

"Sarah likes this stuff. It reminds me of the time me and Daddy had to get up and fix a leak in the roof, and I got all congested from breathin' in the fumes. I had to drink Pa's cough remedy. Remember that? It reminds me of Pa's cough stuff, but, well, she wanted you to have it."

I did remember that. He was sick for days. I wasn't sure I wanted to try it after hearin' that. We all know about Pa's cough stuff. None of us like it none. I haven't a clue what he puts in it, but it'll knock a cold clean out of ya. It's horrible to drink though. Mama knows us kids is really feelin' poorly if we agree to take it.

"Thanks. Thank Sarah for me," I said.

Tommy left my room, and I put the candy on my bed next to a bag Mama had given me. She said it was to carry my important stuff. I didn't really know what that important stuff was, but I figured it would come to me. For then, I considered Tommy's gift an important thing.

Jimmy and Emmy was fightin' over my room most of the day, and Mama was trying to keep the peace. She finally told 'em I wasn't movin' out. I was just goin' on a vacation. They still fought. Only now it was over who would have got it if I was movin' out. It seems to me Mama would have more peace if she'd just let one of 'em have it.

Daddy said it's best just to leave 'em be and fight it out.

"Me and my brothers used to fight just like that. So when we was real little—why before I was even in school—our mama made the room real dark. She put white stars all over the walls and ceilin'. And at night, it looked just like space. If us boys were real quiet, it even sounded like space. It was the first time we ever talked. And after that we didn't fight so much."

Daddy missed his brothers, David and Peter. They was killed in a car wreck out west years ago. David, Peter and Jilly's brother, Ray, had all joined the service. For their goin' away party, they went on a road trip with some of their friends. They had gone to dinner and a show in the city, and then they went to a small club in Rocky Ford, Colorado.

It was a place called The Word, and they heard a new band play. It was a great band, to hear Daddy tell it.

"Zapata's Horse, they called themselves. They played all night long, and the owner even told the crowd they were headed to California to hit the big time."

Now Daddy wasn't there, but his brother, David, called him that night, and Daddy says they were all "high on life after hearing them boys play."

After the concert, they went to a coffee shop and had breakfast. Ray told Daddy they had the best lyrics he had ever heard. They were real impressed with 'em, I guess, and they talked for hours before they left the café and headed back to the hotel.

Ray and his two friends took one cab, and David and Peter took another. Ray said his cab got to the hotel, and he went on up to bed.

"Ray never remembered hearin' any sirens or anything, but when he woke up at noon, the hotel was abuzz with the news of a horrific car crash that mornin'. It was just up the block from the hotel," Daddy told us. "But he started askin' questions of the clerk, and he found out that it involved a taxi."

I guess Ray had a feelin' inside it was their cab since he hadn't seen 'em. He called the police department. The stories were true. That cab driver had worked two shifts and been drinkin' vodka. He crossed into the wrong lane, and a semitruck hit them and forced them into the side of a building. All three people in the cab were killed—the driver and my daddy's brothers.

Daddy always seemed extra sad when he told us they made Ray identify the bodies and call the family and tell them what happened.

"Of course, Ray had to leave for the service just like he planned, but he was havin' a rough time with what happened. They didn't let him go on a ship like he wanted; they didn't even make him go out of the United States at first. They just had him work in the office." Daddy just stopped talkin' then.

"They should have let the man grieve," Mama would say kinda angry-like.

"But he was a good soldier," Daddy said. "He wouldn't complain."

Daddy went on to say that Ray came back one Christmas and told him he was makin' the best of it. Ray said he was still doin' all he could for his country. Daddy said he was just so tired all the time.

They did let him go overseas somewhere, and I guess a couple years later, Ray's wife was having a baby. But she died in childbirth, so Ray had to leave the service and all. Shortly after she died, he got sick too. Daddy said the cancer took him quick after that, but that is all he would say. He can't talk about it.

It makes him real sad even after all these years. Mama says Ray just never got over what happened to my uncles or his poor wife, and he just couldn't fight.

"But he was a good man," she said. "I will never forget what a good man he was."

I have heard Daddy say that's why Jilly is such a gypsy.

"She's just honorin' Ray's memory by traveling all over. She even goes back to The Word every chance she gets," he told Mama.

"That's how she found out the band they saw way back when, Zapata's Horse, was all killed on their way to California," he told her. He added what a shame that was, 'cause they would've been superstars.

On New Year's Eve, I heard Jilly and Daddy talkin'.

"Did you know I went out to the Word a couple years ago? Then I just kept goin'. I went all the way to California. I went to that place Zapata's Horse was supposed to play. It was a nice club. I even saw Elton John while I was there. Ray would have been astounded! It was a great show with lots of energy." She said it so casual.

"What? Elton John? You did not see him," Daddy said.

"Yes, I did. At the Troubadour." Jilly insisted it was true. "He wasn't anybody yet. He only had one song then. And now look at him. You just wait. He is gonna be a huge success. Ya'll wait and see."

Jilly loves music just like Daddy, and she loves finding new music. She even had some music on tapes that she's heard in person.

"I'll play some for ya, Serendipitay. You will love it," Jilly told me.

I was gettin' very anxious to go. We were ready by

mid-January. Tommy had helped Burns load all the suitcases into the bus. Jilly had shopped a lot while they were here, and with the gifts she received at Christmas, she had to borrow a suitcase from Mama to take all her new things.

My suitcases were packed by Mama, so they held a lot. I stood in my room and looked around. Mama had reminded me about my toothbrush and girly stuff. (That curse Becky told me about happened at Christmas. And I was right. I didn't like it none!) I figured out those were my "important things."

I had new books from the library, and I asked to keep them 'til I came back home. Mrs. Wilkins called me honey again, and she said it would be fine. When it came to those books, people called her the Library Nazi, so I didn't understand her sudden niceness. It made me feel kinda creepy. It was like Invasion of the Body Snatchers or somethin'.

Figurin' them important, I put the books in my bag. I looked around my room for other things that were important. I grabbed the camera I got last Christmas, the film I got for my birthday in September, a bottle of perfume Becky let me have, my hairbrush and matching mirror Memaw gave me in secret, and some pictures Max and I developed with the money he got last spring mowing grass.

Max stopped by the day before we left. We were eatin' some of Becky's cookies in the kitchen. He was real sad that I was leavin'.

"Take pictures of everything you're doin' and write me every day. I'm gonna buy a camera with my

Christmas money and do it too." I kept eatin', and he kept talkin'. "You know Miss Allen is gonna make me do projects with Julie Ann Reynolds now."

It was obvious he did not like that idea at all.

"Well, she is way smarter than me. You will get better grades for sure."

"She smells funny, Sip. Like apples or somethin'." He made a face, and I didn't get that at all. Max loves apples.

He stood up from the chair at the kitchen table, and I couldn't believe what he said.

"I guess this is good-bye then." He was lookin' at the floor, and had he not looked so sad, I would have punched him out.

"Don't you dare say good-bye to me, Maxwell Reese Adams!" I yelled. "Don't you dare!"

"Sorry, Sip. Okay, then, I won't."

He walked out the back door just like any other day. As I thought of him then, I realized I would miss him most of all.

I put the pictures in my bag and grabbed the stationery out of my desk drawer. I added a collection of candy in case I got hungry on the bus. Then I grabbed my mood ring, Super Bubble bubble gum Mama didn't know I had, and $3.47 out of my money jar.

I was all set to walk out the door when I remembered the book I found upstairs. In all the excitement, I almost forgot it.

I reached beneath my mattress. I could still feel the grittiness of it. I looked at its cover one more time. I wrapped it in a blue bandana and tucked it into the bag of important things. I decided to have one more talk with God before I left my room.

"Hey. Here I go, right? Now make sure you follow me. I don't wanna have to come all the way back here to talk to ya. Not to mention that probably wouldn't be possible. All this is your doin'. Ya know that, right? And it's right, 'cause if it wasn't right, it wouldn't be happenin', right? Now you just make sure I see the things you want me to see. You gotta make your signs clear. I feel like I have been missin' them lately, and I ain't too happy about it. I don't like just wanderin' through, so if we're gonna do this, you need to make these things perfectly clear, OK? OK. Well then, let's go."

I hesitated. I guess I thought something was gonna happen, or I wished it would or somethin'. I just stood there a second. It didn't feel right to walk away. Not right then anyway. I don't remember thinkin' anything else or sayin' anything. I don't really remember nothin' but just standin' there.

Then I just said, "Okay, then. Thanks."

All of a sudden I felt OK to leave. That was it. I just looked up in the air and said thanks, and it felt right to leave my room.

And that's what I did.

CHAPTER SEVEN

ain't gonna tell ya about the good-bye part. You can imagine with your own thoughts that it was sad. You can probably figure out on your own that Mama cried the whole time, and Daddy just paced around lookin' busy. Honest though, I can't really remember the actual good-byes. I don't like sad stuff, and I especially don't like sayin' good-bye. I think I get that from Max. So you can put your own words in and figure that part out.

Now, I ain't ever left home before. I ain't ever been gone for more than one night. I ain't ever even left my town without at least one of my parents, so I was real nervous. Even though I was comfortable with Jilly, I still felt nervous. Once inside that bus, I sat quiet. I was holdin' onto my bag of important stuff, and I didn't move at all.

I had never been in a motor home before, and it was really strange. It was an old school bus that looked like they had just up and put a house right inside it. I don't know how Burns did it. It had a living room and two bedrooms. It had a bathroom and a kitchen. Now I'm not good at explainin' stuff, I know, but I am gonna try.

When ya first walked in, it looked like a normal

school bus. The door lever was the same, and the driver seat looked just like any other bus. There were two seats right behind the driver, and one on the other side. But that is where the same stopped.

Behind those seats was a wall with a door right in the middle. There was a window in the door with beads hanging on it, and there was a big welcome mat on the floor. When ya opened that door, it no longer looked or felt like a bus at all.

A small sofa was right in front of ya. It was bright orange with big, poofy, yellow, and green pillows. Now we know I'm not one to talk about color, but ya couldn't miss it. The color was everywhere. And I have to tell ya colors detail, or you wouldn't believe me.

There were windows on both sides with tiny white curtains and orange and yellow beads in the middle of them. There was a chair on the left and a fireplace on the right. It didn't have a fire in it, and I wondered if it even could. There were big, white, sparkly rocks all over the front of it and a ledge big enough to sit on. Although, I don't know why you would want to.

There were plants everywhere. They were danglin' from the ceilin' and standin' in big pots in the corners. The walls were light yellow, and the carpet was brown. You read that right. There was carpet!

There were little tables next to the sofa with knickknacks on 'em. It was just like any other livin' room. Behind the sofa was another doorway, but it didn't have a door. I could see through into a small kitchen. There was a table on the right and cabinets on the left.

The countertop had a stove in it, and there was a fridge at the end of the counter. There was another door in the very back, and it opened up into a bedroom. There was a small bathroom on the left side of the room and a bed on the right.

That was Jilly and Burns's room. Joey's room was in the livin' room. That sofa opened up, and there was a bed inside! I was right wonderin' where I would sleep when Jilly showed me the kitchen table folded down, and the seats folded out and made another bed.

Burns had designed the bus himself, and he made most of the furniture. The plants suspended from the ceilin' were in special, bolted pots that didn't sway with movement, and the knickknacks on the tables were screwed on from the bottom. I knew right away why Daddy was so impressed with Burns. He was a real smart man, and it was amazin' what he did to the inside of that bus.

Alabama is only one day and half a night from home, but I was real excited to get there. I wasn't in that bus but an hour, and I wanted to ask if we was there yet. I had to laugh at myself then, and it made me miss Emmy and Jimmy. They sure enough would have asked out loud, but then they would have fought about it after. It made me sort of sad to be leavin'. I had butterflies terrible, and I wondered if that was a connection of some kind. I laughed at myself for that, too.

We headed south. First we went into Missouri and then into Tennessee. We saw where Elvis lives. I took a lot of pictures of that. We never saw Elvis, of course, but it was still fun. He had a big gate on the front of his house with a guitar on it. There were a lot of girls screamin' and yellin' every time a car drove up. We were gonna get out and walk around a little, but Burns really didn't see the fuss.

"It's just a house," he said.

He had a point, I guess. It was not like we was gonna see Elvis himself. But I didn't think it would have hurt to have walked around.

"Oh, yeah. It would be so cool." Joey really wanted to walk around.

But Burns said no. Actually, now that I think some, I don't think Burns said a thing, but Joey just stopped talkin'. I would have done it if I had a kid that wanted to real bad.

Mama loved Elvis, and I can remember Daddy talkin' about him. I remember seein' him in movies and singin' on TV. There was a big show on not too long ago when he went to Hawaii and sang for a bunch of people. They put it on TV, and Mama sat and watched the whole time. I don't think she got up once. I had never seen her do that before.

I thought he dressed funny. And he sure did sweat a lot. It didn't look like much fun really. Just singin' and sweatin'. But then he started smilin'. Then he looked like he was havin' a lot of fun. When he smiled, he looked like he was happy.

I had gotten into my bag twice. First was for my

mood ring, and second was for the camera. After we left Tennessee, I got into my bag for the third time. I took out the pictures of me and Max. I looked through them and laughed at the silly things we took pictures of. There was an empty pop bottle someone sat on a park bench and a lady uptown walkin' her dog, although it looked like the dog was walkin' her. Then there was one of Becky comin' out of her room with cold cream all over her face. She screamed for Mama to tan both of us. I almost laughed out loud. I missed Max. I put the pictures away and got the camera back out.

The trees were different there. They were almost all Christmas trees. They weren't leafy ones like in Iowa. I knew Max would also think that was weird. We have lots of different kinds of trees in Iowa. They are maple and oak mostly. And there's some elm, I think. Max's neighbor has a weepin' willow that we swing on in the summer. But in the south, there's a lot of pine. I looked out the window, and for miles and miles all I saw were trees.

Jilly came into the living part of the bus and sat with me. She said we'd be stoppin' in a while.

"We'll have somethin' to eat and probably sleep a bit."

I guess there was a place up the road. An RV park, she called it.

They had a fire not too long ago, and Burns and Jilly wanted to talk to the people about it. They worked for them sometimes, and they wanted to see they were OK. I was still real nervous about meetin' new people and stayin' in a strange house, in a strange bed, in a strange city with people I barely knew. But I loved Jilly. I couldn't explain it, but I really loved her.

We stopped at Tucker's Ranch. It was sad. There had been a real bad forest fire, and all the trees around the whole place had burned. For as far as you could see the trees were gone. I took a few pictures to show Max.

The owner was an old man named Zeek Tucker, and his wife was Isabella. He called her Ella. They lived there all year long with three sons. They were teenagers like Tommy and Becky. They were busy haulin' away old broken limbs and scoopin' ashes with shovels into an old pickup truck. I felt bad for all of them.

But they didn't even blink an eye when Jilly and Burns asked if we could park a bit. Busy as they were, they stopped and made some coffee. They even sat down and chatted with us. We slept for the night in their burned-out park. Ella sent a care package of muffins and cookies with us when we left the next mornin'.

As we pulled away, I saw them all go right back to work. As we turned onto the highway, they all stopped and waved us on. Even them young boys waved to us, and I wondered if that was southern hospitality like I heard about or just good rearin'. I liked them a lot and hoped it was both.

After thirty-six hours, we arrived in Alabama. Jilly had taught me a lot in the time we were on that bus. Her great-great-grandfather moved here from

Kentucky. He came with his mama, who was some sort of medicine woman. Jilly said she'd tell me the whole story later, but they built their own house from the ground up. It was just outside of town. I guess it's not there anymore, though. It is going to be a shoppin' center. It's even gonna have a new JC Penney there, and it will be part of the town of Bryan.

That was where we were—Bryan, Alabama. The population was 1588. It was a lot smaller than home. There was a tiny grocery store and a barber. There was a gas station and a coffee shop. There was a veterinarian and a police station. Thank God, there was also a library. I was gettin' worried at first. I didn't think a place so small would have one, but it surely did. And it was a big one, too.

I learned a lot about Jilly. Even though she traveled all the time, Bryan was home her whole life. She had moved a couple times. She moved two times during her Red Cross days and once in her twenties. She'd gotten engaged to a man in the army and followed him to Texas for a few months. They never did get married.

Born Elizabeth Jillianna and weighin' only three pounds at birth, she should not have survived. Tellin' me about that, she put it very simply.

"Serendipitay, my life is a miracle, and I am gonna live it like one. There's a reason I was put on this earth, and I am gonna keep searchin' 'til I find it. And if nothin' else, they won't be able to find me if they realize their mistake."

Then she winked and just giggled. I loved her

laugh. It was one of those laughs that makes you laugh back. And then you laugh 'cause it just feels good. And her face would just light up some. She was so beautiful. Like her name.

It was the most beautiful name I had ever heard. There was one thing I didn't get, though. I wouldn't have allowed a nickname if my name was Elizabeth Jilliana. But it didn't take long to figure out that everybody has a nickname down south.

There's a Bubba at the gas station; the barber goes by Honk, and Jilly mentioned Pinky and Flo, the neighbors who collected the mail from the house. I don't know what kind of name Burns is. I didn't ask.

Jilly was different. She wasn't different in a bad way. She was just different. "She marches to the beat of her own drum," Mama always said. Daddy called her a free spirit. To me, she was kooky or maybe even odd. But, she was lovely.

But Jilly was more than all that. She loved life. I could just tell that every day was important to her. She didn't waste energy on things she couldn't change or with people she couldn't reason with. She said once, "Don't argue with a man without reason. It is like givin' medicine to the dead." Then she immediately told me, "Now I didn't make that up. I think Thomas Paine said it, but I'm not sure what he was talking about. From what I read, he was the only one without reason most of the time. But I read he said it once, and I liked it. So now it's just my opinion."

We got to the house late at night. Jilly and Burns

grabbed some of our bags and unlocked the door for Joey and me. I can't explain the house. I can't tell ya what I thought or felt. I just can't. I don't have the words to do that, and words is what I would need to do it right.

I can tell ya it was beautiful. I can tell ya it was like nothing I had ever seen. It was a strange place, but I felt so at home there. There was a smell I can't describe that felt warm. It was like a color I can't name but one so clear. It doesn't make sense to ya, I'm sure, but believe me when I say it was the most beautiful place I had ever been.

I tiptoed as I walked. I felt as if I had fallen into another world like Alice in her Wonderland. I felt light-headed and dizzy but so happy. I had never felt anything like it before. I walked down a hall and into a dinin' room that led to a livin' room.

It looked like how I imagined a parlor. You know, like in Gone with the Wind. I imagined people sittin' on the sofa there sippin' tea.

I imagined a man with a cane and a top hat and a woman in a beautiful dress. I don't know why I pictured that, but I did. That's just how it looked.

I was still tiptoein' when I saw it.

Above the fireplace was a paintin'. It was the most amazin' paintin'. Keep in mind I ain't never seen the ocean. And I ain't never seen a palm tree 'cept in a picture or on the TV on Hawaii Five-O. But I felt as if I was sure seein' the real thing. I stared at it for a long time. I think I might have held my breath at first.

It was of two women and a little girl. Their dresses

were flowin' around their feet. The colors were faint as if they was fadin' a bit. But they were soft— pink, yellow, and light green. They were barefoot in the sand. There was a bench beside them and trees all around. Palm trees. The beach was in the background. There was the ocean and sunlight peakin' through leaves on the trees. A few leaves were on the ground.

The women were smilin'. For a minute, I expected that little girl to move. I expected her to look my way, put her hand to her mouth, and whisper, "Shhhh."

She didn't. But I thought she might. I expected the leaves to start blowin' in the soft breeze, which seemed to be blowin' their dresses just a bit. I expected the wave in the background to roll onto the beach. I expected the women to laugh softly.

I don't know how long I stood there. I still don't have the words right to say how I was feelin'. I never have forgotten it, though. I can sit here right now and see it in my head just like I was still standin' there.

I can even make that little girl run around that bench teasin' those women to chase her. And she giggles. And the breeze blows her blonde hair back away from her face 'cept for one little piece she has to push away herself.

Isn't it weird how I can describe that paintin'? Me. Sippy, who grew up smellin' nothing but fish. (Daddy's gonna like this!)

Jilly showed me to the room where I would sleep. It was a big bedroom across from the dinin' room. It had a tall bed and a fireplace. I found out later they don't have furnaces in Alabama. Can you believe that? So all the houses have lots of fireplaces.

There was wood around the sides of the fireplace, and the mantel held pictures of faces without names. They were young and old, and most all were black and white except for one.

It was a man and woman. She held flowers and wore a colorful hat. It was a weddin' picture I guessed. Next to it there was a picture of a man in a sailor suit. He was young with a nice smile. Mama would call him handsome. Someone had written "Daddy" on its bottom corner. It made me smile and gave the man a personality. Beside it was a picture of two little kids. I figured them about three and five years old.

"I was a cute little thing, wasn't I?" Jilly didn't wait for an answer but went on. "That's me and my brother, Ray." She touched the glass and smiled as she put it back, lining the frame with the dust mark left on the mantel. "We was tiny little ones then." Jilly paused. "Come now, Serendipitay. Let's get some-thin' to eat."

We went off into the kitchen. It was in the back of the house. It was a big room and had big, bulky furniture. A big, rounded sink sat in the far corner. An oversized white stove sat across from it. Burns was there cookin' already. I could smell bacon. We sat down at a big, round, wooden table with chairs that made me feel really small when I sat in 'em.

"Ya like BLTs?"

I said yes even though I didn't like tomatoes. I didn't wanna be rude and all. Jilly started goin' through the mail that had come over the last eight months or so. There was a big box full of it sittin' on a bench next to the table. She tossed most into the trash can but opened a few pieces.

Jilly, like I said, didn't look her age. Her long hair was always pinned back outta her eyes, and she wore little makeup. Her skin was like a doll's. It was real soft lookin'. And even late at night and after travelin' all that way, she was just as pretty as ever.

She read Burns a couple things she opened. One was about insurance, and another was about a rally goin' on in Texas in about a month. She threw away the insurance one. Jilly had turned on the old radio that sat to the left of the stove; Pa had a radio like it in the garage that didn't work anymore. Jilly's did. She turned it up.

It was shaped like a triangle, and the music came out of the bottom. There was a fast song playing. I liked it. The man singin' was talkin' about him and a girl named Susie.

It made me think of Daddy. I thought of him and Mama holdin' hands. I didn't ever remember them skippin' stones, but I suddenly missed them both very much. I could hear Daddy now, singin' the song to Mama and her rollin' her eyes and shakin' her head at him.

It made me smile. I listened closer to the song and the man singin'. I really liked it. It was fun, and I could hear the piano real good. It made me want to get up and dance, even though I didn't know how. Jilly liked it too. Suddenly she was so excited!

"That's him! I told you. Elton John. I saw him play that piano in California! I knew that night he'd be on the radio!" She was jumpin' all around.

I liked the voice. I liked the piano. I would never forget that name! Next thing I knew, the music was up even louder, and she was dancin', right there, around the kitchen.

"Come on, girl. Let's dance." She held her hands out, and we was dancin' all over the kitchen. She grabbed a nearby mop and started dancing with it. She was twirlin' and twistin' and singin'.

She wasn't using any words. She was just singing na na na, but she made it fun. I had never danced before, but I wanted to try.

"Don't worry, Serendipitay. There is no one but us watchin'."

I followed Jilly and did what she did. There wasn't much to dancin'. Ya just moved your feet faster than walkin' was all. And you jumped a little every now and then. And then you turned around a couple times. It was so fun!

Burns never joined in, but Joey did. Him and Jilly were twirlin' all over the place. It was just like what I had seen on TV. Joey was good, and I knew Jilly had taught him. I had never seen anyone dance in the kitchen before. It was fun, and I was so glad I came with them.

After we ate and cleaned up the kitchen, it was time for bed. We were all real tired, and Jilly had a big day planned for us. We were gettin' up early, and we were gonna go see the town. I didn't figure that would take long, the town, being as small as it was.

"You will be gone all day," Burns said. He appeared annoyed.

"Oh now. Not all day," Jilly said almost as a defense.

"Yeah. We'll see." He sounded like he was challengin' her.

It was a strange conversation. I still couldn't imagine it would take all day. However, I was learnin' quick that Jilly didn't do anything fast 'cept dance. So we said our good-nights, and off to bed we went.

Smilin', I climbed into my bed, which I would like to point out was the softest bed I had ever been in. I thought about the few hours I had been there. I smiled at the thought of me, Jilly, and Joey dancin' in the kitchen, of the warm I felt in the house, at the paintin' above the fireplace, at the tour of the town I would get tomorrow, and of the two things in life that were now my favorites—BLTs and Elton John.

As I snuggled down into the covers, which I would like to point out were the softest covers I had ever felt, I had my first Alabama talk with God.

"Hey. It's me, Sippy. Sorry for whisperin', but I don't wanna wake anybody. Thanks for bringin' me here. And thanks for lettin' me dance with Jilly. And, hey, why didn't you tell me how good BLTs were? And that Elton guy? You did good with that one. Watch over Mama and Daddy for me, OK? And Tommy, Becky, Jimmy, and Emmy. Yeah, you know. And watch over Burns and Jilly, too. And Joey. And me. All right. Well, good night." I snuggled into the blanket, and before I closed my eyes, I added, "Oh, and one more thing. What is this bed made out of? It's fantastic! Good night."

With that, I slept better than I ever had.

CHAPTER EIGHT

MAMA called bright and early the next mornin' to see how I was gettin' along. I told her she shouldn't worry about a thing. Mama is so funny about stuff like that. She reminded me to brush my teeth, and she told me to say please and thank you. She said she missed me, and then she asked to talk to Jilly. I gave the phone to her and went back to my Alabama room.

Jilly had given me the drawers in the old dresser and half of the big armoire closet. She said I could use the secretary desk too. I arranged all my books first. Then I put some more film into my camera, put some things in the drawers, and sat down to write Max a quick letter. I kept it pretty short.

Dear Max,

Hi. It's me. It's real nice down here. The house is real pretty. Still don't know about my real parents. No clues yet.

Took pictures of Elvis' house. (Will send them next time.) Have ya heard that Elton John guy on the radio yet? He is pretty good. He is real good at piano. And he can sing too. And have you ever had a BLT? They are real good. Black licorice is not.

See ya later. Sippy

I addressed the envelope and stuck a stamp in the corner. I stuck my stationery back into the cubbyhole in the secretary desk. I looked in some of the other drawers. There were more old pictures and an old postcard I couldn't read anymore. There was so much history. There had to be clues here about my real parents. I just had to find them. I looked around the room.

There was an old trunk. It was bigger than the one at home. But it was full of blankets and sheets. And there were moth balls too. That's a smell for ya. Whew! There were two closets. The smaller one had shelves on each side, and there were more books and a lot of boxes.

I picked one of the boxes from the top shelf. Inside it was a hat. It was a really big straw hat. It had a bunch of purple and yellow flowers on one side and a brighter yellow ribbon going around the top. It was really colorful. I wasn't sure who would wear a hat like that. I bet it was even bigger than Minnie Pearl's, and I always thought that was a pretty big hat.

I laid it carefully back in the tissue it was packed in and placed it back on the shelf I found it. Still snoopin', I found more hats. They were similar in color and style, but they were all slightly different. All were very big. All were very colorful. Someone really liked hats.

Mama never wore hats much. Memaw would wear a hat on Sunday when she went to church, and Mama always bought us girls hats to wear on Easter, but Emmy was the only one of us who still did. Still, I ain't never seen hats like these. Shoot, most of Memaw's hats would have fit inside any one of these. I laughed a little and thought of dressin' up in them hats and how Becky would have giggled seein' it. I missed her then.

I could hear Jilly and Burns in the kitchen. I figured they was gettin' ready to go into town. As I started out of my room, though, I could hear a difference in Burns's voice. It was stern and loud. It startled me, and I waited to join them.

I sat back on my bed. I could not hear words at first, but I could tell he was mad about somethin'. Jilly's voice was different too, but I couldn't put my finger on how. I would have waited forever, but before I knew it, Jilly was at my door peekin' in and sayin' it was time to go.

She was different somehow. She was quiet at first. I didn't see Burns anywhere. I was about to ask when she announced it would just be the two of us in town. I didn't mind none, but I thought it was strange. I thought it was strange that the house seemed so empty and quiet. We gathered up our jackets and headed out.

When Jilly and I left out the side door of that old house, I looked back. From the upstairs window, I saw Joey lookin' out. He just stood there and watched us go. Then he waved a short, quick wave. I felt bad. Somethin' inside me knew he wanted to go. I waved back. Then I saw Burns in that window too. And I could have sworn Joey jumped. Then they both disappeared behind the curtain.

So Jilly and I spent the day in town. I met Bubba from the gas station. He was a funny guy. He told me all about him and his family.

"I always wanted enough kids for a baseball team. Well, I'll be darned if the first three and the last two were girls. I ain't got nothin' but twelve kids." He laughed so hard at himself he got to coughin' and had to take the cigar out his mouth so he could spit some. I liked him, and not because he gave me a strawberry soda out of his machine, but 'cause he was funny and real nice.

Then we went and ate at the coffee shop. Thelma was the waitress there, even though her name tag said "Babe." She dates the guy at the barbershop. They call him Honk. I don't know why, and I didn't ask. She made me a big cheeseburger and fries and I think the best chocolate malt I have ever had.

Jilly took me to the town square, and we sat on a bench by a statue of an army soldier. She told me the story of her great-great-great-grandmother, Anna Lovett, and how they all came to live there.

"She was a medicine woman, don't ya know, and she had ten children. Now, she was a widow, Serendipitay, and it was unheard of back in those days for a woman to travel unattended. But she did. She was a strong woman." She winked then. "That's where we get it. And she was smart." She pointed to our left. There were no houses, but it was the path all the settlers took back then. "Those kids and her built a small shop just west of here. They set up shop to doctor anybody who passed through.

"She would accept clothin' for the children, food, or animals as payment. Before she knew it, she had people comin' from miles away for doctorin'. Some paid her with services and lumber.

"Her kids worked and built 'em a house from the ground up. It was just two miles outside of town. Other settlers soon joined them. It wasn't long before they had a little town." She stood as she spoke, and she walked closer to the statue until she was straight in front of it.

"Her oldest son, Bryan, my great-great-grandfather, joined the army and became a war hero. That's how the town got its name, Bryan. And that new shoppin' center—why, it's gonna be called Lovett Center. They named it after her. After us, Serendipitay. After our family. You know, Grandmother Anna lived here her whole life. She was doctorin' right up to the day she died." She smiled as she spoke.

It was an impressive story, and Jilly told it with such enthusiasm and love. You could tell when she talked that she just loved where she came from. It made her proud to be who she was. Listenin' to her made me proud. She would refer to our ancestors as our grandfather or grandmother. It was a great day. I kept forgettin' they weren't my ancestors. They weren't my family. How could I keep forgettin' that?

We stopped at the post office and mailed my letter to Max. Then we went by the grocery store for a few things before headin' home. The house was just as quiet as when we left. Joey was out back with his bicycle. It was in pieces all around him. He had tools, and he looked like he was doing somethin' real important.

Jilly made us hot tea, and we went to the parlor room. She continued to tell me about the family. We went through pictures and old letters. It was so much information, and my mind was soakin' it all up. I loved it.

I heard Burns come into the kitchen, but he didn't stay. Soon he headed to the garage. He just didn't seem right to me. It wasn't like he was watchin' me or nothin', but it was more like he was waitin' to get mad at me for somethin'. I can't rightly explain it, but that's how it felt.

I was never disrespectful, mind ya, but I didn't talk much to him. He didn't scare me exactly, but I didn't want him talkin' stern to me like I heard him talkin' to Jilly. In fact I didn't want him talkin' like that to anybody. I just made sure I didn't say much at all. I think Jilly must have had the same thoughts 'cause when he was around, she was real quiet too.

Joey was the only one who really talked to him, even though Burns never talked back much. He usually just gave him somethin' to go do. It wasn't like chores or nothin', but he was always tellin' him to go ride his bike or go fishin'.

Just anything to get him out of his way it seemed. I felt bad for Joey. I can't imagine my own daddy not wantin' me around, and that's sure how it seemed for Joey. But Joey would just do as he was told. I think he was afraid of him some.

From that day, I discovered two things. One, my

mood ring wouldn't turn any color but black, and two, I had a real uneasy feelin' about Burns.

I threw my mood ring away.

CHAPTER NINE

TIME went quickly, and Jilly kept me busy learnin' about family. I met a lot of people. They were mostly friends of Jilly and a couple distant cousins. Burns and Joey kept to themselves mostly, separately of course, and Burns was only around durin' meal-time. It was strange to me, but it seemed normal to them.

Jilly and I read from the old books in the house. We read book after book of poetry, short stories, and novels. We read the poetry of Dickenson, Frost, and Poe. We read stories by Charles Dickens and E.B. White. It thrilled me when I realized that book on grammar I had was also by E.B. White.

We also read Hemingway. It became a ritual at night after supper to read a page or two from The Old Man and the Sea. I loved listenin' to Jilly read, and the story became one of my favorites. Even Joey sat with us a couple of nights when Burns wasn't around to make fun of him or tell him to go to his room.

Mama made sure to call once a week. She worried about me, I knew. I had been there just over a month when she called one afternoon. Jilly had sent some of my assignments home, and Mama called to say I did real well on a math test. I loved hearin' her voice. She said it seemed like forever since she saw me.

"I miss seein' your eyes every day, Sippy." I thought it was funny 'cause Mama never talked to me like that before. It felt good to hear.

She told me Tommy and Sarah had both joined the missionary group that would be going over to Paris in the fall, and Emmy won the spelling bee at school. Becky liked her job at the Dairy Mart, and Daddy discovered four new things to do with tinfoil. I didn't ask. All she said about Jimmy is that he missed me.

Memaw was doin' fine, and Aunt Lily was back visitin' from Oregon, so she was helpin' out a lot. I was glad for that. She said she couldn't wait to see me again and hoped I was having a good time and enjoyin' bein' with Jilly. It made me miss her something terrible. Later that night, Jilly saw I was homesick, so I got the full Johnson house tour.

"Come on, child. It's time you meet the house."

She knew so much. She knew dates and times and names. I told her she would have to write it all down for me sometime 'cause I wouldn't remember it all. She promised she would.

"I'll do just that. I have journals I write in every day. I'll be sure to write one for you." She made a mental note as we went upstairs.

The upstairs had been shut off years ago 'cause she didn't need the space. She was born there and had lived in it her whole life. She showed me her old room. It still had the vanity she would use to get herself fixed up for school.

"See these old iron tongs? I would heat them up in the oil lamp and then wrap my hair around 'em." She demonstrated. "The heat would cause the hair to curl. Then I would take a burned match and charcoal to make a beauty mark right here, on the corner of my mouth." She pointed to the spot right by her dimple. "By the time I was done I looked like a gypsy princess. I always did have some gypsy in me, even as a small child."

Her twang made her words go up and down like she was singin'. And she winked and smiled as she always did when she amused herself.

We ended the tour in the parlor. We looked through family pictures. She told me stories of the people that were in them. The wedding picture I saw was of Daddy's parents. I knew they had died long ago. Jilly said her mama told her they were real good people.

"They had five children in all. Your daddy, his two brothers, David and Peter, and twin daughters, Victoria and Mary," Jilly continued. "When your daddy was about five or six, they had a bad house fire. Only he and his brothers survived. Of course, we were family, so they immediately came to live here. My daddy was their daddy's brother.

"Now my parents had three children of their own, mind ya. There was me; my brother, Ray; and our baby sister, Eva." She became quieter then. "Quite a houseful, it was."

Jilly was just starin' off.

"Jilly?" I asked. "What's wrong?"

She smiled then and told me her baby sister, Eva, died shortly after that from polio at the age of two.

"I was only three, and I don't even remember her none. It makes me sad. I try so hard to see her face. But I can't. So I imagine her as an angel with beautiful, golden wings. I imagine her lookin' down." Jilly's face brightened as she spoke. "And then she sees me right back. And she spreads her wings real big, and they glisten like they have diamonds in 'em."

Jilly smiled and was lookin' up. I knew by the look on her face she was seein' those wings then.

Jilly is real good at describin' things. When she talks, I see exactly what she is seein'. I told her that night I could see Eva too. I saw her just the way she said. She told me all the angels look like that, and if I ever miss someone who has gone to Heaven, I can sit back and imagine them like that.

"And then they will spread their diamond wings for you to see." Jilly smiled, and her eyes sparkled. I'm thinkin' it was a reflection of the angel wings she was seein'.

I didn't know anyone in Heaven yet, but I told her I would remember that. I decided then would be a good time to ask Jilly about God.

CHAPTER TEN

"**J**ILLY? Do you talk to God?"

"God?" she asked.

"Yeah, do you talk to Him?" I asked again.

"God is everywhere, and each person on earth has a different idea of God."

"I mean the God in Heaven. Do you talk to him?"

"Honey, we all have spirit guides. Some call that guide God. Some don't. It's a personal thing. I know what ya mean, though, and although I might not call mine God, the answer is yes," she said matter-of-factly.

"It's like prayin' though, right? Is it the same as prayin'?" I asked her, but I wasn't sure if she would understand.

"Yes, I suppose it is." She thought a moment. "Yes, it is prayin'."

"Does he talk back to you?" I watched her closely then.

"You mean are my prayers answered?" She shook her head a bit. "You know darlin', the answers come in different ways. Sometimes we get our answers and don't even know it."

"No. I mean does he talk to you? Like in a real voice." I hesitated. "I heard a real voice talkin' to me." I still watched her. She didn't look shocked or alarmed.

"Oh, Serendipitay! The voice you hear is your own."

"Oh, no ... " I started to explain. But she continued.

"Those are the spirit guides who live inside you, honey. Those are the voices ya'll hear. All the spirit guides speak in one way or another, and they sometimes use us to get their messages out."

"So, it's not God? What about the signs? He talks to me, and then I get signs too." I felt very comfortable talkin' to Jilly.

"Because of who you are, it's God. He is your spirit guide." She looked at me with a softness I saw often.

"When he shows you a sign, honey, that's faith. That is your faith believing in what he has told you."

"But sometimes I don't understand," I confided.

"You don't always have to understand, Serendipitay. Sometimes you never will. I never really understood why my brother was taken from this life. I don't understand why I could never have a child of my own. There are things we are not meant to understand. We must believe it is what is best."

"But then, why does want even exist? Like you not havin' children. Why did he let you want children if you couldn't have any?"

"Well, let's see if I can explain this." She scooted closer to me on the parlor sofa. She rubbed her hands together and slapped her knees once. She leaned in close. "Want cannot be controlled. Have you ever been in a pizza place and wanted a hamburger?" I nodded.

"Me, too. Right uptown. That pizza place couldn't control what I wanted. But it couldn't give me a hamburger, either." She continued without faltering. "But those folks up there made me the best pizza I have ever had. And I ate that pizza and absolutely loved it!" I nodded slightly, even though she didn't wait for that.

"They gave me a place to eat it, and the nice people who brought it gave me everything necessary to enjoy that pizza. They couldn't make it a hamburger, though I loved it just the same. And even though I still wanted a hamburger, I wouldn't have been able to eat one right then 'cause I was full up from eatin' great pizza. See?"

I smiled at her and understood what she said.

"Our spirit guides cannot control our wants, honey. They can only control how we deal with those wants. They can give us strength to love what we have. They give us the ability to be thankful for all the things around us that makes us happy."

"But how do you stop wantin'? Doesn't it make you sad?"

"Yes," she said. "It can make me very sad, if I let it." She talked slower now as if she was thinkin' real hard. "People will always want. There is nothing we can do to stop that. Even the spirit guides can't stop us from wantin'. But you can control what you want." She sat up real straight then. "I don't want to be sad. I want to be happy. I choose happy. That is somethin' the spirit guides and I can give me. And that is my faith."

Her face lit up in that Jilly way before she added, "I find things in life that make me happy. Music makes me happy. Writin' in my journals makes me happy. Family makes me happy. Friends, flowers, the sun, and the sky make me happy. Even rain and puddles make me happy. Hats, butterflies, and the smell of lavender—all of that makes me happy!"

She was beamin' with joy.

"Lavender?"

"Yes. One day not too long ago, I suddenly smelled lavender. I don't rightly know where it came from. Maybe it was a neighborin' garden, but it was the most glorious smell. It relaxed me as soon as I smelled it, and it made me smile the rest of that whole day!"

She was still smilin', and I found myself smilin' too. Right then, I knew my life was exactly right. No matter what. It didn't matter if Mama and Daddy weren't my real parents 'cause they were still my mama and daddy. I knew I was guided there to find my place, and this was it. I was meant to find the meanin' of love, and I had. I was meant to find the joy of family, and that was in Jilly. I was meant to find the existence of God, and that was in me. I'd learned so much and was so grateful.

What I didn't know was how much more there was to learn. But I was about to find out.

CHAPTER ELEVEN

SINCE I had been with Jilly, I had a greater love of music and books. I had heard about the highs and lows of life and death. I learned love is inside us always, and if we are willin' to risk bein' hurt, it can be wonderful. I learned more about faith and how it is in each of us but different for everybody.

I learned God was the same. And while some don't call Him God like I do, it's OK. I learned that talkin' is still prayin'. It's what each person thinks and believes it to be. As long as it's for the sake of good, it's right.

I also realized there's a voice in all of us. It talks to each of us and talks through us. And there's one that guides us. I learned all of our beliefs, hopes, and dreams are challenged each and every day. It's how we deal with those challenges that makes us who we are. And it's who we are that touches others in our life. Jilly also taught me that while we can sometimes challenge each other, we also bring each other good. All of this is what gives us strength, faith, love, and happiness. The challenges we face make us strong. I was about to face one of those challenges.

One mornin', while Jilly and I had tea and toast with sugar, she talked about her mama. She smiled as she talked about her. She truly loved her with all her heart.

"I write everything down, darlin'. I keep a journal of all my thoughts, wishes, and dreams. Even talks with my spirit guide sometimes come out in what I write." She walked over to her desk and pulled out a book.

It was a brown leather book with gold flecks on it. It was old, and the pages were yellowed. She sat it on the table in front of me.

"This is my great-grandmother's journal." It wasn't just any book. It was exactly like the one I had found in our attic. I picked up the book and held it in my hand. I could feel the grittiness of its cover. Tears came to my eyes. She looked confused.

"What's wrong, honey? Why you sad, Serendipi-tay? This shouldn't make you sad, darlin'."

I got up from my chair—the one that made me feel so small. I went and got my bag from my room. As I walked back into the kitchen, I pulled out the blue bandana I had stuffed into the bottom. I handed it to Jilly.

She looked into the cloth and pulled out the book I had hidden there. She gasped.

"Where did you get this?" she asked. She looked at me with eyes I had never seen before.

"I found it in the attic at home."

"But … " She stopped talkin', and I didn't know why.

I showed her the card and the inscription. I showed her the date.

"That's my birthday. The people that wrote this. Are they my parents?"

She looked at me with a look of happy sadness. I don't know how else to explain it. The tears that filled her eyes rolled down her cheeks slowly.

"No, honey. Jonas and Eliza are my great-grand-parents. The little girl they are referring to is my grandmother. They shared this with each other the day she was born." She opened the book, held it up to me, and pointed. "September 10, 1862. Exactly one hundred years before you. See the date there?"

It wasn't about me! I almost felt silly. I laughed a nervous laugh that made the tears in my eyes come out. But somethin' still didn't feel right. Jilly continued to cry.

"Honey, where did you get this?"

"In our attic." Jilly still looked confused as I explained where I had found the book. "It was in an old trunk in our attic."

"Okay, honey. We need to call your mama and daddy." She seemed frantic.

I could tell there was somethin' wrong. I could tell by the way Jilly stood up but didn't move. I could tell she was nervous about something.

"No. Why do we need to call them? You tell me. What is it?" I was scared for the first time since I'd heard the voice.

"Serendipitay, I need to call yo—"

"No! You tell me! You tell me now! Memaw told my mama I needed to go with you. She knew I needed to be here. Now you tell me why!" I yelled at Jilly for the first and only time in my life. And I was cryin' harder than I ever had. "You tell me!"

"Oh, Serendipitay. You are so young. And your mama and daddy love you so." Her tears were like mine. There was no stoppin' them. I could barely talk anymore.

"Tell me." It came out as only a whisper.

"OK, I will tell you. You are adopted."

She said the day I was born was a beautiful day. Both my parents were so excited for me to arrive. She said my mother had been feelin' festive and more energized, so she knew I was on the way.

"Jilly, your mother said. I am energized. This baby is comin'! She had been on bed rest for months, and I had helped ready your nursery. We called all her family to tell 'em to be ready. She had me call on your father and tell him to be comin' home." Jilly chuckled a little, and I wasn't sure why.

"I knew it would take a few days for your father to get a message and even longer to get home. But I sent it as she asked, and we hoped he would get it on time."

"Where was he?"

"In the navy," she said. "And your mother sometimes forgot he couldn't just leave." I realized that was why she chuckled. "Needless to say, he didn't make it home before you came, but he called that mornin'. I told him what you looked like, and he cried. He was so happy. He asked me to get your mother a present. A special one, he said. Get her somethin' real special. So I did. I went into my mama's room, and I got this book." She held up my book. "This book, which my great-grandfather gave my great-grandmother on the day of their daughter's birth."

She held the book as if it were the most breakable glass in the world. She caressed the cover with the tips of her fingers. She continued to talk.

"It had the inscription that matched you. It matched you and your parents. Your mother and father could have written that inscription, honey. You looked just like my grandmother the day she was born." Jilly looked at me and touched my check. "You had light eyes like your mother," she began to cry again. "And you had light hair like your father— my brother, Ray."

CHAPTER TWELVE

I had come to Alabama for the truth, and as much as I wanted to know it, I wasn't expectin' what I was hearin'. Jilly got up and walked into my room. She came out carryin' the picture of that handsome sailor. It was the one with the name "Daddy" written in the corner.

"This is your father in his uniform." She handed the picture to me. "And this is your mother." She held before me a photo of a woman with blonde hair. It looked soft like wheat flowin' in a field. She was like a doll. Her skin was flawless. She was beautiful.

"Both of these pictures sat by your crib in your nursery." She looked at the pictures with me. He was handsome, and I liked how he smiled. Jilly sat next to me at the table. She continued.

"Honey, by the time I got back to the hospital, your mother had taken sick. Real sick."

Jilly told me how she laid that book on her bedside table and waited for her to wake up.

"The nurses were in and out to check on her. They even brought you in to see her. They placed you in her arms and told her you were there. She knew you were there. I just know she did. She was so peaceful when you were with her. But she never did

111

wake up." Jilly held her hand out, and I took it into mine. "Late the third night, she just died. Real quiet and peaceful."

I closed my eyes then and tried real hard to see her. I knew she had blonde hair. I tried to see and remember her. I tried to remember being a baby and feelin' myself in my mother's arms. I couldn't remember.

I shut my eyes real tight then, and I pictured the woman in the photo as the most beautiful angel I could. She had golden hair and sparkly, golden wings with diamonds. And there she was. Just like Jilly said she would be. She was beautiful. And she smiled as she spread those wings for me to see.

I looked up at Jilly then. She was cryin' and looked so sad.

"Please don't be sad," I said, and she pulled me next to her. We sat there for a bit and cried together. We got up from the table and took our tea to the parlor.

Jilly continued to tell me that my father didn't even get to see my mother. He got home the day after she died. Jilly told me that Ray was lost without her, and he didn't know what do.

"But he was in love with you. Oh, how he looked at you. I'd never seen that kind of love in all my life."

Jilly said she helped all she could. She stayed with me.

"But he was so tired. He could barely get outta bed some days. And he cried a lot. Never when he held you, though. He loved you so very much.

"The navy, you see, had been doctorin' him for the sadness from the accident so many years before. But this was more than that, so I took him to a doctor here in Alabama."

But it was more than anybody knew. The doctors told Jilly just how sick he was.

"It was more than sad. He had a cancer in him. It was all over. He didn't have energy to fight it none. He was sick. Those doctors in Birmingham said it'd been in him a long time. They said it was just a darkness throughout his whole body. They said he'd just be gettin' worse. They didn't give him but six months to live." She wiped away tears that rolled down her face. "I couldn't take care of him and you too."

She told me how she got him a nurse.

"One of them navy nurses came and lived at the house and took real good care of him. The navy was so good to us then. They took care of everything we needed.

"You stayed with me, in your room now, and your father was in the back part of the house. It was the part we built for my mama when she took ill. We visited him every day. He would hold you and sing to you. He tired easily, and you often fell asleep together." She brought out some pictures she had in the desk. I could see my little face peekin' out of the blanket lying in the elbow part of his arm.

"You must have been about four months old when he asked me to call Jack and Suzie."

"Why did he ask you to call Mama and Daddy?"

"See, when your father found out he was sick,

he called your daddy, Jack. He and Jack had always promised to take care of each other's families. Being in the navy, my brother always worried about that. We had all grown up together. They were like brothers. He asked for them when he knew it was time."

Jilly told me that Ray wanted them to be my parents, as he knew she couldn't do it.

"I was a gypsy at heart, and he knew that." She laughed just for a second. "My brother wanted the best for you, and he knew you would get it from Jack and Suzie."

She told me how my daddy and mama cried when Ray told them it was time. She said Mama and Daddy fell for me the second they saw me. She said Daddy cried again when Ray asked them to be my parents, but they didn't hesitate a second to say yes.

"So your brother, Ray, was my real father? Who was my mother? What was her name?"

"She was my brother's high school sweetheart. Her name was Serena, honey. That is why your daddy, Jack, tried so hard to name you. He wanted to honor your mother with a beautiful name. He said you were a surprise blessing from God." She smiled and shook her head. "Now don't think we weren't shocked when he named you, but not one of us was gonna change it 'cause Ray loved it!"

"But I was four months old. Didn't I have a name before then?" Jilly laughed. Tears were still streamin' down her cheeks, and more were fillin' her eyes.

"Just Sippy."

"What?" I looked at her, but I didn't understand.

"When your father got to meet you, the nurses asked him what he was going to name you. He didn't take his eyes off you for even a second. He just said, 'Sippy'. The nurses, of course, thought they heard him wrong and were confused. They asked him again, and he replied, 'Sippy. Just Sippy.' So for four months we called you Sippy. We never did know why he chose that name. I never asked, and he never told me."

She looked like she wished she'd asked.

"When your mama and daddy came and named you Serendipity, they took you in to meet Tommy and Becky. Becky took one look at you, and in an effort to say Serendipity, it came out Sippy. 'Course we all thought it was fate."

She said my father was at peace after that, and he just smiled and closed his eyes. Five days later he passed away.

"He didn't say good-bye. He never wanted that. The last thing he said to me was, 'See ya later,' just like he did every day." Jilly looked down at her lap for a long time. She didn't say anything. I could tell she was cryin' again. "I have loved you from the day you were born, Serendipitay. You also came into my life by accident. You took me places in my heart that I will never go again." She looked up at me. "I will never have children of my own, and I will never experience motherhood in the way most do. But for four short months," she took my hand in hers, "I experienced the closest thing to motherhood I ever will. I will forever be grateful to you for that."

She wiped her tears and looked me right in the eye. I felt complete like I never had before.

"Your mama and daddy have loved you like their own. They have never thought of you as less than that. You know that, right?"

"I know," I said, and I truly believed her.

"They wanted to tell you when you were old enough to understand."

"But … " I stopped. There wasn't a "but." I wanted my parents.

"Can I go home now?"

"Yes. We'll get you home."

"Jilly?"

"Yes, honey?"

"Thank you," I said, "for everything."

"Aw, honey. Don't thank me. You are my pleasure and my favorite." With that, she winked, and I saw that Jilly smile I loved so very much.

"I love you." I paused. "Aunt Jilly. I love you."

"I love you more, Serendipitay," she said as she hugged me. "More than you'll ever know."

I went into my room then and thought about packin', but I decided I had to talk to God one more time from Alabama.

"Hi. It's me. This has been quite a day. So you have my parents up there? You better take good care of 'em. And they best always have the shiniest wings, ya hear? I mean it now. And make sure whenever it's my turn to come there they're the first people I meet!

"In fact, you just need to keep all my people in the same place, so everybody's all together."

I tried hard not to cry as I talked to Him.

"Now, I don't get why they had to come there like they did. I don't even want to know that. But ya did good leavin' me here with Mama and Daddy. And with Jilly. Ya did good with all the family you chose for me. They were all a good choice. They've been real good to me. So, thank you for that.

"Now, you gotta do me a favor, though. You gotta make Jilly happy. She has done good. And I know she's got her own thoughts on bein' happy, but ... just give Jilly some happy. OK? Well, thanks again. I bet you're glad I know the truth now, so life can go on, right?

"How's that work, anyway? Life goin' on, I mean. How? What do I do different? Do I do anything different? Great! Now ya got me all full up on more questions I can't answer! And let me guess. I will figure them out on my own, right? Well, you're still gonna help, OK?"

I waited for the invisible answer and then just finished as always.

"OK. Thanks. Good night."

I smiled. I always make sure I smile. Actually, I think it just comes natural. I never have to fake it, so it must.

I packed my things into my suitcase. And I organized my bag of important things. Jilly had given the book back to me. She said she doesn't know how it ended up in my hands, but that is where it would stay now. I wrapped it back in the blue bandana and carefully placed it in my bag.

I heard Burns come in the house as I got into my pajama's. I didn't hear him speak to Jilly, but I could hear him in the kitchen. He wasn't a very quiet man. He slammed a couple cupboards and clanged together some dishes. I heard Jilly ask him to be quieter so as not to wake Joey and me. All I heard after that was the back door slam.

I drifted off to sleep with an uneasy feeling. I would realize the next mornin', I should have talked to God about Burns.

CHAPTER ~~THIRTEEN~~
FOURTEEN

THE next mornin' Jilly told Burns of our talk. She told him everyone would be goin' back to Iowa. Burns didn't like that we was goin', I guess. I could hear him from my room as I gathered up my things. I knew he was gonna start yellin', and I didn't like it none.

I don't like violence, but I went to the kitchen anyway. He was getting louder and louder. I started to get kind of scared. I still can't say in words what that felt like. I had never heard anyone swear like that before. I mean, sure, I heard people say damn and even hell. But some of his words I didn't even know. As I stood in the kitchen doorway, he looked at me. I never had anyone look at me like that before.

The veins on his neck were bulgin', and his forehead was red, and his skin looked real tight. His eyes were all bloodshot with little red veins in 'em goin' every which way. And he was scowlin' like he ate somethin' real bad. He was even pinchin' his lips together real tight and grindin' his teeth 'til they made a sound.

He was breathin' so heavy it was like he was chokin' on somethin' and couldn't catch his breath. His hands were balled up in fists, and he was bouncin' on his feet. He bent his arms up and then back down to his sides. Over and over. Swingin' fists! Veins bulgin'! Teeth grindin'! Heavy breathin'! Frownin'! Scowlin'!

The growlin' sounded like hate. It was just meanness was all—pure meanness. And then he was yellin', and his face was so red it was purple. He was swearin' and yellin' so loud it hurt my ears. And it was mean. Just mean. And it made me jump. Spit was comin' out of his mouth. And I jumped again. I just wanted him to stop. I would have done or said anything to get him to stop, even if it was saying I was wrong and he was right. That is what Jilly did all the time—until that day!

Right then, Jilly stood up to Burns. She looked him right in the eye and told him she wasn't afraid of him anymore. She told him the hate and the meanness was over. And she was stern. She wasn't mean. She was just very matter-of-fact. Like I said, I never have liked to hear people fightin' or yellin', but what was about to happen I wasn't expectin' at all.

The next sound was breakin' glass, and it filled the air. Jilly gasped, and another loud shatter made me jump. I ran back to my room as fast as I could.

What followed was a loud slammin' sound and more screamin'. I could no longer understand his words. There was more slammin'. It was like when the teacher slaps the yardstick on the desk. Only it was louder, as if he was using a door instead of a three-foot ruler. This went on and on. I figured Burns was madder than he'd ever been. What would make him so mad about me leavin'?

I heard Jilly tell him I knew everything and wanted my parents. I heard her say I was just sad and wanted to go home. I didn't hear his response. I just heard his anger. He was just so mad. There were more slammin' sounds. They came again and again. And then there was silence. Eerie silence. I didn't hear words. I didn't hear anything except myself take in a breath. I had been holding my breath since the first sound of glass. I listened closely at the door. There was nothin'.

Then I heard the sound of a car start. Its engine was loud, and its tires squealed some, and then it all faded away.

I opened the door slowly. I could hear faint sounds of glass clangin' together. I quietly made my way toward the kitchen. I could hear Jilly then.

She was hummin' softly a song I didn't recognize. She was sweepin' up the coffee cups and plates that had broken on the floor. There was coffee spilled as well. She looked up as I came into the room. She apologized and said she hoped the commotion didn't scare me too badly. I told her it didn't.

I grabbed a towel and helped her clean up. She looked tired and didn't have that Jilly sparkle. She didn't offer an explanation. She didn't say anything. She just continued to sweep and hum softly within herself. Then she asked if I was hungry.

I was and didn't deny it. We ate our normal breakfast of hot tea and toast with sugar. We talked of Mama and Daddy. She had called them early and told 'em we were comin'. She told them I knew about my parents.

"They said to tell you they love you and can't wait to see you."

"They weren't mad, were they?"

I wasn't sure why I asked that 'cause I knew in my heart they weren't. Jilly confirmed that. She said they asked how I knew, and she told them of the book I found in the attic. They told her about the trunk.

It had all my baby things in it that they took from Alabama. They intended to tell me this year, and Mama had dug the trunk out to go through it. She wanted to give me the things in it. They told Jilly with Memaw getting' sick and all, they waited to say anything. They promised to talk to me as soon as I got home.

She didn't say a word about Burns. Neither him or Joey was anywhere in sight. I finally asked, "Is Burns comin' with us, Jilly?"

"No." That was her only reply, and it was very matter-of-fact.

We cleaned up the rest of the kitchen together. She still hummed that same tune. We packed our things in the bus. We walked up to town and said our good-byes to Bubba and Honk. And we stopped in for a cheeseburger and fries from Thelma. Jilly called her Babe this time. I had what was the second best chocolate malt I've ever had.

We left for Iowa after lunch. I didn't know it, but

the trip would teach me more about life and love than I already knew.

CHAPTER FIFTEEN

JILLY and I talked on the way home. She wasn't sad like I thought she would be, but she was different somehow. She said Burns wasn't taught how good and bad go together and that love takes work. He wasn't taught hard work or sacrifice.

"He was a selfish man with his love. He was even that way with his own child. We butted heads about that a lot. He wouldn't talk to Joey much, and he would yell at me when I tried to have a relationship with him. He said I was gonna make Joey a sissy if I babied him. I didn't baby him. I just wanted to talk to him. He hated that I taught him to dance."

"That is so sad. I feel bad for Joey."

"I told him it's important to love children when they are little. That way, they know what love is and what it feels like. They know how to love back." She wiped a tear. "But he wouldn't hear of it. He said his mama left him when he was eight years old, and he turned out just fine." She shook her head. "He don't even know how he is."

He thought the world owed him, she said, and it was hard to get around that side of him.

"I tried to love him and make him believe in the good. But that was all so new to him. He didn't believe in the good of anything. There was always something bad that had to be first. Always. He thought if people feared him, they respected him. He didn't know the difference.

"We fought about that too. And when he fought, he hated. You couldn't disagree with him. It had to be all or nothing. I loved him with all my heart, honey. I would have gone to the ends of the earth for him, but love is the whole package, ya know?" She didn't wait for me to answer. "It's not about what you have or don't have. Somebody still has to take out the trash, and ya gotta love 'em even if they don't."

I thought about Tommy and how he would be in trouble if Mama stopped lovin' him every time he forgot to do that.

"There is always gonna be responsibility. Life is hard, and you have to work. And you don't always get what you want. Some people hate that. They run from it, and they resent it. Then they think the love is lost. They think they fell out of love."

She wasn't cryin' anymore, but her voice was quivering. She continued to talk.

"I have come to realize over the years, honey, that when love is real and you are committed to one another completely, you can disagree and even argue. You can have hard times. You can do without things you want. And you can struggle. It's all OK. You gotta stay your own person, but you are also one together. And ya gotta be there for each other, no matter what. And ya may not understand each other all the time, but ya gotta try. Sometimes ya can't fix what ya want, and sometimes ya can't undo things that are done. But it makes you stronger. It is supposed to make your love stronger."

She was so true to herself.

"Love cannot be lost, stolen, or fallen out of. When you love deeply, truly, and unconditionally, nothing else matters."

"Wouldn't he want to be different?" I asked. "Burns, I mean. Wouldn't he want to be a good man?"

"That's the trouble, honey. He thinks he is a good man," she said, "but his mama is in him good. And he just runs away.

"I had to let him go this time." She glanced over at me. "I had to let it be."

She turned on the tape player and I heard the song she was hummin' in the kitchen. It was by the Beatles. She told me to listen, so I did; I listened to the words about lettin' things be and about waitin'. I listened to how answers will come if you just wait.

I thought about my talk with God the night before. I thought about my question about life bein' different. I felt, right then and there, He was usin' that music to tell me it was gonna be fine. I felt it was Him tellin' me to shine on until tomorrow and just let things be.

Jilly played music all the way home. She played more of the Beatles for me to hear. I loved the music. She told me about all the Beatles. She told me about George Harrison and Ringo Starr and how Paul McCartney and John Lennon wrote most all the songs. She told me how they was real famous for it.

She played me songs by John Lennon. I listened to the words of "Imagine." It was the best song I had ever heard. I wanted to write like that. I hoped I could learn. Ringo was her favorite; I could have guessed that. John Lennon was mine.

Other than talkin' about music, Jilly was quiet. For most of the trip I watched out the window and felt the urge to write things down. I wanted to convey what I saw in words. As she drove, I took out my camera. I wanted to remember so I could write about it later.

I also took pictures of things I knew Max would like. There was a fancy sports car at a gas station in Tupelo, Mississippi, a nice view of the Missouri River, and the St. Louis Arch. I missed Max and wanted to tell him all I had learned. I wanted to share my new music with him. I wanted to tell him about my parents.

I wanted to see Tommy and hear him whistle. I wanted to see Becky and watch her brush her hair. I even wanted to hear Emmy bossin' Jimmy around.

I was ready to be home. And I needed to talk to my mama and daddy. I figured there was more they wanted to tell me.

I was so right.

CHAPTER SIXTEEN

WE got home late, and Daddy must have carried me in 'cause I woke up in my own bed. At first I was thinkin' it had all been a dream, but then I saw my bags and knew it was real. I looked around my room and smiled at the thought of bein' there. I talked with God that mornin', but all I said was, "Thank you" before runnin' down the stairs to find my family.

I went down to the kitchen and saw Mama and Jilly sittin' at the table. I went over and hugged Mama so tight I thought I might break her. She had been cryin'. I could tell. There were balls of tissue all over tabletop and in her hand, too.

She had her coffee sittin' in front of her, but it was full up. Have you ever noticed when grown-ups are busy talkin' their coffee just sits there and gets cold? I noticed that about 'em. And I'm bettin' my mama's coffee was cold then.

We didn't say anything. She just looked me right in the eyes. I could tell it was love comin' out of her. She brushed my hair away from my face a little. And she held my hand. We didn't have to say anything at all. We both knew. I loved my mama so much right then. No words could have come outta me anyhow.

There was that feelin' in my throat. You know, the one when you're gonna cry, but it doesn't come out. And it hurts kinda but not like strep. It's different than that.

It's like there's somethin' stuck. Ya can't swallow. Ya can't talk. Ya can't do anything. And your jaw starts to ache. So ya just wait. Ya wait for that to go away so you can talk. Or swallow. Or even cry. 'Cause that there feelin' in your throat stops ya from cryin' even.

I couldn't talk. I couldn't swallow. I just waited while I looked at my mama. She must have had that feelin' too. She didn't talk. She didn't swallow. She just waited like me. We hugged again. As my heart felt her arms wrap around me, I cried.

And that feelin' in my throat drifted away real slow. The tightness that was gonna choke me was gone. That ache in my jaw went away too, and I could finally talk.

I looked up at Mama, and she was cryin' too. What I said came out in a whisper.

"I love you, Mama."

"I love you, baby daughter." She patted my back and rubbed in little circles. "Now run and find your daddy. He's missed you terrible."

Daddy was outside, and I grabbed some juice on my way out the door. He was standin' in our driveway mendin' the fencin' at the very end. He looked up when he heard the screen door slam. He put down his tools and took the handkerchief outta his back pocket.

Now he couldn't have been sweatin' none in forty

degrees, but he wiped his forehead anyhow. I saw him kick the dirt a couple times as I walked up. He looked up for a bit like when I talk to God. I even thought I heard him curse a little. I was sure he was cursin' at the sky more than God.

"Hi, Daddy."

"Walk with me, Sippy." He put his arm around my shoulder. "Your mama and I was given a gift from Ray. You weren't just a child. You were a gift. And we will never forget that."

That was the first time I saw my daddy cry. But he wasn't sad.

He turned, grabbed me up into his arms, and held me so tight.

"We loved you so much. From the minute we looked at you." We started walkin' again back the way we came. "And that love has grown so deep and strong."

"I love you and Mama too. More now than ever. And I've missed hangin' out with you. Do you remember how we used to play baseball up at the park?"

"I do. That was fun."

"Remember when that man thought I was a boy?" I laughed and nudged him.

"Remember? Of course, I remember." He turned to face me and stopped walkin'. "That felt worse than the day the music died. I lost my little girl that day." He wiped his dry forehead again. "After that, you just grew up."

We were back at the start of our fence.

"Oh, Daddy." I hugged him tight around the

waist. "I'm still your little girl. Why, even when I'm old, like forty, I'll be your little girl!"

I hugged him tighter, and he hugged me back. Then he laughed. He held me out at arm's length then.

"Hey, now. Forty ain't old!" He picked his tools back up. "Now let's get busy. You can help me with this fencin'."

I laughed too, and we fixed the rest of that fence together. He even let me hammer some. And when we got all done, Daddy said I did good work.

We gathered up our things and started up our drive for the house. As we walked, I looked up at Daddy and saw that smile. You know the one. It was the one he has when he talks about Mama. Or music. Or baseball.

Sure enough, I saw it right then when he looked at me.

We got everybody together for a nice lunch and told them the truth. We looked at old pictures of my parents and heard stories about when they were young. Daddy talked about workin' in the shipyard and bein' on a freight.

He had pulled that old trunk out of the attic. In it were some of my father's books and pictures of him. Some were ones he had taken himself. They were nice pictures, and I loved seein' them. We looked at each item and carefully placed it back in the trunk.

There was a small, silver box with a rose attached to the top. It was carved out of what looked like marble. Mama handed it to me. I opened it slowly.

Inside was a small heart-shaped locket. I opened it carefully and found that same picture of my father in his navy uniform.

"Your mother wore that every day," Mama said as I held it in my hand and looked at the picture inside.

"It's beautiful."

I put it on.

There was cameo pin that was from Jilly's mother. She had given it to my mother as a wedding present. There were letters my father had written to my mother that I decided to read later.

In the bottom of that box, folded perfectly, was a delicate handkerchief. It was the thinnest, softest material I had ever touched. I could see it was white, even though time had dulled it some. It was still beautiful. Green leaves of ivy bordered all the edges, and clusters of smaller ivy filled the middle. It looked like somebody had hand painted every single leaf.

As I unfolded it, I could smell a faint trace of perfume. It was soft and sweet. I closed my eyes as I inhaled a big breath of that sweet smell. It was a smell I recognized. Lavender.

Once again, I saw in my mind that golden-haired angel with diamond wings smilin' down at me. Smilin' myself, I carefully folded the hankie as perfect as I found it, and I laid it back in that little, silver box. I kept that box with me as Daddy continued through the contents in the trunk.

He pulled out a little, wooden shoe. Jilly laughed out loud when she saw it.

"Oh, I remember that! It was made in Holland.

He brought it for you, and he was so proud of it. It was filled with chocolate." She laughed louder. "I told him, Ray, I said, that baby can't eat chocolate! And he just shrugged and said he bought it for ya, anyway." Jilly apologized then for eatin' the chocolate. "It was the best chocolate I ever had, though!" she said and giggled again.

I told her I didn't mind, and we all laughed.

Everybody laughed 'cept Jimmy. He just sat there most of the time. His head was lookin' down into his lap. He hadn't said a word the whole time. Suddenly, he stood. He walked toward me. He stopped right in front of me. Standin', he was eye level to me. He looked me right in the eye. He was serious.

"I was right! All along, I was right! You're not my real sister!"

And with that he ran off. He ran as fast as he could out of our livin' room, through our dinin' room, into our kitchen, and out the back door.

I ran after him. I knew where he would go.

I went out our back door, over the mini-creek, up Johnson Mountain, and down the other side.

I found Jimmy down in the gully. He was just sittin' there on that old tree.

I walked up, sat down next to him, and decided it was a good time we both had a talk with God.

CHAPTER SEVENTEEN

WE just sat together on that old tree. Neither one of us spoke at first. I decided I would speak first. But I spoke to God.

"Hi. It's me, Sippy." Jimmy looked confused at first. "This is Jimmy, but you know that."

"Who you talkin' to, Sippy?" He looked over his shoulder and around the back of me like he expected someone to be there.

"Jimmy. Say hello to God." I motioned to the sky. "Go ahead, and don't be rude. Just say hello." I motioned again into the air with a little wave of my hand toward Heaven.

"Hello?" he said slowly.

It was more of a question than a salutation. (I learned that word in that writin' book I'd been readin'. Pretty good word, huh?)

"We are here 'cause, ya know, Jimmy don't think I'm real." My speech was very matter-of-fact. I was beginnin' to notice a lot of Jilly in me, and I rather liked it.

"So," I continued, "I'm gonna explain somethin' to him, and if I get it wrong ... well... you can just make lightnin' strike this old tree again!"

"Sippy!" Jimmy yelled.

"What?"

Now I knew I was doin' two things. First, I was takin' a real chance at makin' God mad enough to strike that tree good. Second, I was gettin' Jimmy to talk. I had faith in both those things.

"Don't be sayin' stuff like that. God will strike us for sure!" he said. "Besides, I know you're real. You're just not my real sister is all."

"Well, I have faith He won't strike us, and you just need to listen." I shushed him and continued my talk with God. "Now when you took my mother and father up there to Heaven with ya, I know you had already picked who my new parents would be. My guess is you knew that long before you knew you needed them in Heaven." I stopped and waited a second. "I must be right so far," I said to Jimmy, and then and I giggled a little.

He just shook his head and slowly put it into his hand. He was sweatin', I could tell. And he might have been prayin' a little on his own too. I smiled up at God.

"So there I was in this new family. I was their new daughter. I cried. I laughed. I ate. When I fell down and skinned my knee, Mama kissed it and made it better."

Jimmy stopped me. "I said I knew you were real! I know you cried and stuff."

"Well then. Why ain't I your real sister? Is it 'cause my parents are different?"

"Yeah."

"Well, he's wrong, ain't he?" I asked God. "Ain't it

right that when we're born into families we are daughters and sons, but we're also brothers and sisters?" I didn't wait. "I know when you chose Jimmy to come into our family, he came into it as my brother. Ain't that right?"

"But, Sippy—"

"There ain't no buts here. This is a talk with God, and there ain't no buts about that."

I motioned to God with my index finger to hang on. Yep, right then and there, I told God to hang on a minute. I knew he would, and I turned to my little brother.

"Jimmy, I was your sister from the minute you were born. That ain't any different. And Tommy, why, he was born to be a big brother. And Becky, she's the best big sister ever. They were born that way. And it don't matter who our parents are or who they're not. The fact is we are brothers and sisters, and that won't ever change." I looked back up and included God again. "Ain't that right?"

I knew it was right. Jimmy just sat there thinkin' for a minute.

"So we're keepin' her, right?" he asked as he looked up to God. And then he turned to me. "He ain't gonna answer for real is he?" he asked in a nervous whisper.

"No. He's not." I had to laugh about that. "But I know what He would say if He did." Remembering Jilly's words, I felt God more than ever, and I felt him speak through her. "Love each other deeply, truly, and unconditionally. After that, nothin' else matters!" I lifted Jimmy's chin so he looked at me. "Then he would say, 'Heck yes, you're keepin' her!'"

He jumped into my arms and hugged me around my neck. I looked up and thanked God over Jimmy's shoulder.

He was never mad after that. We went back home and joined the rest of the family. I looked at Mama and Daddy and winked; they knew it was all right.

Becky found out a couple days later that Jimmy had found that old trunk long before me. He and some friends had come up with a story you would only hear in the movies.

Not only did they think I was gonna get taken back by my scary, evil parents, but somewhere along the way, the information got so mixed up that the whole town thought Becky was with child and lookin' to adopt it out. I guess Mama was right about gossipin'.

As for Jilly, she, of course, remained a free spirit and couldn't stay with us long. She was plannin' a trip up to Minnesota to see her friends, While and Linda McCann. Daddy told us they were the sole survivors of the crash that killed that band Zapata's Horse. I remembered, then, that Joey told me he met them once. He said their boy could play guitar real good. She loved it up there, and the McCanns had become like family to her.

Now I had changed a lot, but one thing remained. I didn't like good-bye. I avoided Jilly all mornin' the day she was fixin' to leave. Tommy had helped her load her bags, and Becky had helped Mama pack her a snack. Daddy checked out her house bus, makin' sure it was fit for travel. Even Emmy and Jimmy were close by to help with small stuff.

She came up to my room right after lunch.

"You avoidin' me, Serendipitay?" she asked.

"Yes," I said, using my matter-of-fact "Jilly voice."

"I'm gonna be writin' you all the time, now. It'll be like we're right together."

"But we won't be. We won't be together."

And right then I got that feelin' in my throat. It come over me quick and hurt like never before. My throat and jaw were so tight I thought for sure I was gonna choke to death this time. I kept my head down. I didn't look up. I didn't move.

Jilly walked over and sat on my bed right beside me. She took off one of her beaded necklaces and put it around my neck.

"You keep this, child. It is me, with you, all the time." She touched each bead as they dangled on my chest. "And even when you are too old to wear it, and it sits alone in an old jewelry box, it'll still be me, with you." Her voice trailed off to a whisper then, and she held out her hand for me to see. On her left ring finger was my mood ring. "I know you threw this away at my house. Well, it's blue on my finger, honey. And that's where it'll stay. It is you, with me, all the time."

That feelin' in my throat was unbearable, and the tears wouldn't stay in any longer. I sobbed uncontrollably into her chest as we hugged. She was hard and soft all at the same time. I didn't wanna let her go. But I knew I had to, so I did. I walked her downstairs and out to her house bus. She said her farewell to the rest of the family, and then as she pulled out our driveway, I heard her yell, "See ya'll later."

I watched as she turned off our road and drove outta sight.

Knowing the truth didn't change me. It didn't change us. It made us closer. It made us stronger. And we didn't know it yet, but stronger is what we were gonna need to be.

CHAPTER EIGHTEEN

AFTER Jilly left, life went back to normal, though it would never be the same. Max and I went to the library, and I told him all about my parents. We looked up information about Bryan and Anna Lovett. He was obsessed with the army after that.

"That's what I'm gonna do, Sip. I'm gonna go to the army and get a city named after me."

He stuck his chest out, and he walked all stiff down the aisle of books.

"You gotta go to war and be a hero first. You ain't gonna be no war hero, Max."

I didn't mean to burst his bubble, but I think I did a little. But not too much. That's all he talked about from that day on.

I got a letter from Jilly the next month sayin' some tornadoes ripped through Ohio and Indiana the week before and delayed her trip to New York. She was makin' the best of it, of course, and enjoyin' her visit with the McCanns. She said she was just gonna stay and help in their store all summer and head to New York in the fall.

She was high on life as always. She asked what Daddy thought of Hank Aaron breakin' Babe Ruth's home run record. I wrote her back right away.

Dearest Jilly,

Hope you are well and enjoyin' your visit with the McCanns. Tell them hello from me and that I hope to meet them someday.

Daddy said baseball will never be the same. However, his thoughts may be because girls are allowed to play Little League now.

Tommy and Sarah are engaged to be married, and Becky wants to join the Peace Corps. Mama is happy about one but not the other. Can you guess? Emmy joined the glee club. She is really good at singing.

Oh, you know that camera I had? Well, I gave it to Jimmy, and he is outside every day now taking pictures of anything that will hold still. Mama says he has found his calling.

As for me, I am really trying to learn to write better. I enjoy it very much and have been reading up on it. This letter is my practice. How did I do?

I miss you so much, but I am so glad for the time we spent together. Please write soon. Send pictures.

Love always,
Serendipity

Now, I never felt like a child after my time with Jilly. I can't rightly explain it none. I felt so free inside and yet so confined at times. It was like I was gonna bust. I can't rightly explain that either, but it's true.

I went to visit Memaw for a weekend just after Jilly left. We talked about the way I was feelin', and she explained the best she could.

"Your mama always said you had a 'look in your

eyes,' Sippy. She feared that really. She always felt like you would be missin' something we couldn't give ya." She didn't wait for me to comment. "Suzanna! That's what I call your mama when I'm bein' serious with her, ya know. Suzanna, I said, you love her the best ya can. You give her strong wings and a strong spirit, and when the time comes for her to fly, you let her. And with the pride of a mama bird, you watch your baby use the wings you give her."

"Is that what I'm feelin'? My free spirit? My need to fly?"

"It's part of it. But when that time comes, child, you won't have doubt. You'll just take off! All the big things in life are like that. It's like love, Serendipity. That's what I call you when I'm bein' serious. When you find love, there won't be any doubt." She patted my knee and smiled. "That conflict inside you is what growin' up feels like, and you are growin' up mighty fine. I'm real proud of ya."

I felt closer to Memaw after that, and I understood Mama a little better too. She was my mama bird, and I knew I had strong wings. I promised myself right then and there that I would fly high someday and make my mama proud.

Summer school started, and of course, Mama and Daddy made me go. Emmy was in glee club over the summer, and since Becky got a new truck, she got to drive us. We all became closer, and Becky even started teachin' me about doin' my hair and makeup.

First time Daddy saw that he said I was pretty just the way I was.

"Oh, Jack. Makeup isn't about bein' pretty. It's about growin' up." Mama winked at me.

He must have listened to her. He didn't grumble when I wore it anymore. I remember one night we were going to Emmy's recital. Becky helped me get ready. When I was all fixed up, Daddy looked at me and smiled.

"Your father told me once you were like a fine wine—one he wanted to savor and just sip. Later he said you were a fine wine he couldn't finish. But still, he said you were like a sip of the best wine ever made. That's why he called you Sippy, ya know." He cleared his throat and stood up. "And I don't know a lot about wine 'cept that it gets better with time. He was right about you bein' like fine wine, Sippy. You look real pretty."

"Daddy, I never knew that story before. Thanks for tellin' it to me."

We all went to Emmy's recital, and she did good. She smiled as she sang. She danced, and she looked so happy. We were so proud. And we talked about it all the way home. Daddy said he was gonna teach her some guitar chords.

The phone was ringin' when we come in, and Mama ran to answer.

"Hello? Oh no! I'm on my way!"

Mama ran into the livin' room and said she was runnin' to the store. Daddy went with her. I knew she lied. I didn't hold it against her then, and I don't hold it against her now.

I sat in our living room in an old rockin' chair.

I didn't move. I knew somethin' was terribly wrong. Even ol' Whiskey knew something wasn't right. He just sat there with me. His tail was quiet on the floor, and Whiskey never did that. He didn't lick on me like usual. He just sat there with his head on my knee. If I didn't know better, I bet he couldn't swallow. We both just waited.

I fell asleep in that chair, and Mama woke me up when she came in. I could see she had been cryin'.

"Where did you go, Mama?"

I sat up some, but I was still sleepy. I hoped she would lie.

"Memaw's."

Tears filled her eyes, and I felt that tightness in my throat and jaw.

I stared Mama down, willing her to lie again. I didn't speak. I couldn't see her face anymore 'cause my own tears were fillin' my eyes. I didn't wanna blink them away. I didn't wanna see my mama's face. I didn't want Mama to talk. I didn't wanna hear any more. I closed my eyes and felt the tears on my cheeks.

I could taste the salt as they crept in the sides of my mouth, even though I kept my mouth shut as tight as I could. I kept my eyes closed and wished it would all go away.

I stared into the darkness of my closed eyes. I saw her then. Her eyes were smilin' like they always did. And she was pretty as ever with her diamond-studded, golden wings spread wide for me to see. I saw Memaw as a beautiful angel in Heaven as I heard Mama say, "She didn't make it, Sippy."

CHAPTER NINETEEN

I am not gonna go into the sadness we all experienced with the passin' of my grandmother. It just wouldn't be right to share that here. I'm also not gonna share the talk I had with God about it. Some things are just better off private. I can say this. I grew up fast after that. We all did.

In the fall, Jilly left Minnesota for New York just like she said. She had written often just as she promised. Daddy was strugglin' with a lot of things, but it was namely our government. So he had started watching the news and going to town meetings.

"Only a well-informed man can have an opinion worth statin'," he told us at dinner. "You all need to remember that."

We promised we would.

By the end of the year, President Nixon had resigned, and Jilly had discovered the Ramones. Elton John recorded "Lucy in the Sky with Diamonds," and I loved him more than ever before.

"Music and politics will never be the same," Daddy said, and I agreed.

In the summer of '76, of course, we celebrated America's two-hundredth birthday with a big family picnic, and in the fall we celebrated my fourteenth birthday. Jilly sent flowers; Mama made my favorite supper, BLTs; Becky fixed me a chocolate cake; and Max bought me the new Elton John album, Here and There. I was disappointed, though, as the duet with John Lennon from the concert at Madison Square Garden wasn't on it, and that is what the "There" stood for. I still loved it, but I was disappointed.

That same year, Aunt Rosie got a CB radio. Mama thought for sure she was gonna marry Stan, "The Ice Cream Man.", a trucker from Arkansas.

"No man should be allowed to have that much hair on his arms when your poor Daddy don't have any on his head."

Mama had a unique way with words sometimes.

Thankfully, though, Rosie didn't marry Stan. But she did marry a salesman from Decatur. His name was Bert. Rosie said his bein' a salesman was close enough to an "S" for her.

Mama thinks the idea of bein' married to a hairy man named Stanley Redd scared Aunt Rosie half to death. I laughed out loud when I thought how close my aunt came to bein' Mrs. Rosie Redd.

As for the rest of the family, Tommy and Sarah married around Christmas, and they both went off to college on the east coast. Becky joined the Peace Corps and will be moving to Spain soon. Emmy, Jimmy, and I are doing well in school and getting along great. Jilly writes often and even visited once on her way to Montana. When she was fixin' to leave, Daddy teased her about settlin' down.

"Why on earth would I do that?"

Of course, he didn't have an answer, so she smiled, got in her house bus, and went to Montana. Our relationship continues to grow. We learn something new about each other all the time. And we have an ongoing battle of the bands. Each one of us believes our music is the best. I know, deep down, her punk rock existence is only skin deep. Rock and roll is in her heart.

In the fall of '77, I was up at the corner store. It was the month school was to start. I had gone up to look at some writing paper I wanted to get. I remember bein' up at the counter when the news came on the radio. I can remember just standin' there with everybody in that store. We were all just starin' at that radio, waitin' for that announcer to say somethin' different. Not one of us could believe what we heard.

I left that store and ran home fast as I could. I skipped every other step on the new deck Daddy built, and I didn't stop to take off my shoes when I ran in the back door. I found Mama sittin' in the living room. She was watchin' the TV. She heard it too.

She had tears streamin' down her face, and I felt so helpless. I went to her and hugged her, and she sobbed into my shoulder. I told her how sorry I was, and although I didn't understand how sad she was, I knew it was a huge loss for her. It was awful, and the world of music would never be the same without Elvis.

I called Jilly that night, and we talked about his death. Jilly had a way of describing things that made it easier to understand.

"There's an energy missin' now, Serendipitay. An unexplainable presence is gone, and that kind of void is without words or understandin'. You can't dwell on why. You can't change it. You grieve. You cry. Then all you can do is let it be."

After that, it seemed as if the whole world went crazy. Television took over the family, and family time became TV time. Mama hated that. The news became filled with negative thoughts and stories of death and destruction. Daddy hated that.

As for me, I focused on school and my writing. I was gonna change the world with my words. I loved learning, and I tried every day to find something I didn't already know. Jilly and I wrote all the time, and she tried to call once a week. She wrote me once on her way to a silent retreat. I wrote her back and asked what that was, but she was already there, so she couldn't talk. She wrote me a couple weeks later and explained.

My Dearest Serendipity,
    I apologize for not communicating with you these past two weeks. I went up to the mountains in South Dakota and cleansed my mind of all its impurities. I couldn't write you back, as we weren't allowed to speak while we were there. I didn't like that at all.
    My body will have to grow toxic, as I love talkin' way too much.
    Love always,
    Jilly

I continued to be amazed with her passion for life. Jilly was approaching fifty years old, and I hoped with all my heart I would have that same passion at fifty.

Passion is what I strove for, and as the decade ended and a new one began, I had questions about life and growing up. I went to God with most of them as well as my parents. Any other questions I asked my teachers.

Learning became my passion and my focus. I wanted to learn everything there was to learn. I wanted to write about what I learned. And then I wanted to learn some more.

While most of the world was asking, "Who Shot J.R.?" I was trying to figure out quadratic equations and dangling participles.

And then the unthinkable happened.

Someone killed John Lennon.

CHAPTER TWENTY

I, like John Lennon, had imagined a better world. And as I looked at life with the eyes of a heart-broken dreamer, I was still determined to conquer all obstacles.

As I turned eighteen and we elected an actor president, Daddy proclaimed, "Look out world!"

I'm not sure which of the two events worried him more.

Next spring, of course, was graduation. In spite of my instructors' attempts to stop my use of passive voice, completely unnecessary indulgence in way too many filler words, and a consistent yet annoying array of both run-on and incomplete sentences, I had become known for my poetry and short stories. They started calling it style, and that was an honor I took very seriously. I graduated at the top of my class.

I was filled with wonder and passion as I entered the real world, but I suppose I had my head in the clouds a bit. I had no idea what to expect. I had a zest for life instilled in me since that fall of '73 when Jilly walked into my heart and set up residency. She and I had spent a lifetime filled with love and joy. We talked of all our trials and tribulations. We helped each other, encouraged each other, and loved each other.

I suppose I looked at life through her rose-colored glasses.

But life became quicker after high school. Max joined the army, and life became robotic. Life became real. I studied journalism, and over the next ten years, my generation saw a rock star bite the head off a bat, the space shuttle explode, and Sonny Bono become mayor of Palm Springs.

Daddy said it again. "Music and politics will never be the same."

Jilly and I continued our relationship, celebrating in '86 when Buddy Holly, the Everly Brothers, and Elvis made it into the Rock and Roll Hall of Fame. She came to visit and brought some of those hats I loved so much. We dressed up in them and danced all around the kitchen. We took pictures of each other and had Daddy take some of us together. I felt so free.

At twenty-four years old, I felt as if I was still eleven. I sent Max copies of the pictures.

Another year passed, and more changed.

Albums became CDs, Pete Rose was banned from baseball, and Jilly got a car. In '88 the Beatles entered the Rock and Roll Hall of Fame, and I got married. Now you would think all that happenin' so fast would have made us all crazy, but it didn't.

Even Daddy hung in there. He didn't make a joke about politics or baseball, he didn't cry when he gave me away, and he even left Jilly alone about her sixteen-year-old "new" car —a '72 Dodge Dart. He did wear a baseball cap with his tux, though. Mama just looked at him standin' outside the chapel.

"Oh, Jack!"

But it didn't make him take it off. I thought he looked real handsome.

The wedding was short and sweet, but it opened the door for children. And that is how I brought in the 90s. Five times! That's right. I had five children—all in the 90s.

At the birth of my first child, a son I named Reese Winston, Max sent the ultimate gift. It was a rerelease of that beloved Here and There album, which included the songs Elton sang with John Winston Lennon.

Max reenlisted in the army, and he was stationed overseas somewhere. I hadn't seen him in years, and I only heard from him a couple times since he shipped out. His mama and daddy had moved to Arizona in '88 on account of his mama's health, and I don't think he had been back since. He enclosed a note with the album.

Hey Sip,

I can't believe you had a baby. And I really can't believe you named him Reese. And what the heck is Winston? He is gonna get made fun of bad. You can't even nickname that mess. I'm still stationed overseas, but I can't say much more than that.

When I make it back, will have to teach that kid of yours to stand up for himself. He's gonna need all the help he can get. Say hi to your folks.

Max

That note and the births of my other children

JUST SIPPY

were the highlights of the 90s. From violence in the Olympics to a baseball strike that cancelled a World Series, the 90s were challenging. News footage of the police chasing a white Bronco changed sports forever, Michael Jackson and Lisa Marie shocked the music world, and the Oklahoma bombing left the entire country in dismay.

We started caring more about what our presidents didn't do and less about what they did. Phones were in our cars, and computers were in our homes. I remember when I asked Jilly if she wanted to get one so we could e-mail.

"I checked into that," she said. "I went right uptown here. We got us one of those fancy stores now." She was excited about their new Walmart. "I had 'em show me one," she said, "and I gotta tell ya, honey. The only thing I drive is my car, memory is somethin' I'm losin', and a wizard is who Dorothy went to see. I don't do windows, and I don't want a virus!"

She giggled at herself as always, and then she rattled off somethin' about being too old.

I had never heard Jilly say the word old before, and it sounded out of character. She went on to say she bought a bike and would be riding it instead of driving because driving was starting to make her nervous.

I continued to raise my kids in a digital world, worked for the local paper, tried to save my failing marriage, and developed a new fondness for John

153

Cusack, Dr. Pepper, and country music. (We won't tell Jilly or Daddy that last part.)

Jilly had stayed close to home since 1997, and she had an increased interest in everyone's family history. She even asked for my husband's information in her last letter. Daddy said she was making sure we weren't related. I told Daddy that being related can't be all bad.

"Dottie and Frank Roberts's crazy kids grew up to be the best acrobats around. They even had their own show in Vegas for awhile."

Daddy just laughed, and I told him I would call Jilly. That night I did call her. We talked about our life—past and present. I told her of my kids' new way to dance. It involved sprinkling baby powder all over the kitchen floor. She laughed at that but said she'd likely break a hip if she tried it.

We talked of family. We talked about my job at the paper. And we talked about my marriage. She told me if I had doubt I should talk to God.

"Serendipitay," she said, "you have the best spirit of all to guide you. Talk to your God, and you will no longer have doubt."

And then she told me she had Parkinson's.

CHAPTER TWENTY-ONE

AFTER talking with Jilly about her disease, I felt numb. I didn't know much about Parkinson's disease except the actor, Michael J. Fox, had it. And I knew there was no cure.

I called Daddy and told him about Jilly. I called While McCann and his wife, Linda, and I spoke with them. They loved her like family, and they promised they would write and try to visit. I told them she would like that a lot.

Then I just thought about Jilly. I thought about all the things in life she had taught me. I thought about what she said about doubt. I thought about what she said about God.

Although my relationship with God had not changed over the years, I will admit, there were times I didn't talk to Him when I should have. I knew I had not been talking to God lately. I had been asking for things from God. I was asking when I should have been talking.

I was asking Him to soften my husband's heart. Every night as we fell asleep, I would lay my hand upon his back and ask God to enter him through me. I had promised God I would never give up. I would never leave. I begged for a softened heart. I even bargained for it.

I thought about Memaw and what she had told me years before about love. She said there is no doubt with love. I was full of doubt. I had been doubting my marriage, my God, my faith, and myself.

That night as my husband and I went to sleep, I talked with God. But I didn't ask for what I wanted. I asked for what He wanted. I asked Him to decide. I asked Him to change what He wanted changed. If that was not the man He wanted for me, then He and only He could change it. I gave it all to Him, and I told Him my life was in His hands.

And then I spoke to Him about Jilly, but that will remain private.

I thanked Him for everything.

As always, I kissed my husband on his shoulder, and then I laid my head there and fell asleep. I was hoping it would get better. It didn't.

Two months later, he was gone. He just packed his things and left. No explanation. Nothing. He just looked at me, said I deserved better, and drove away.

I knew then that God had decided. It was done. And just like Jilly did so many years before, I let him go.

CHAPTER TWENTY-TWO

MY kids and I have been on our own now for seven years. We have made a great life for ourselves. We have been through some tough times, and they have made us stronger. We share a love for music and books that was instilled in me many years ago.

Max never came home from the army. My letters started getting returned unopened. I tried to call his mama, but the number I had was disconnected. After four years, I sent one last note.

Dear Max,
    I will always love you.
    Sippy

That letter didn't come back, but I got a note from someone else.

Dear Sippy,
    He loved you too.
    Sincerely,
    Captain Mark Lawson
    United States Army

I cried when I read it. I called Daddy, and Mama and I prayed together. I talked to God later, privately, and I cried some more. I wanted to write back to Capt. Lawson but decided against it. He told me what he wanted me to know. I let it be.

"Good-bye, Max," I said that night after I talked with God.

I have stayed in Iowa in the same town where I grew up. While I'm happy, there are times I wish I could be like Tommy and Sarah, who live a typical yuppie existence in New York with their English bull-dogs and two homeschooled kids. Or like Becky and live in a foreign land. Mama said last week Becky met a nice minister, and Mama's sure she will be announcing an engagement soon. Or like Emmy, who has her own country rock band now, and although she's not on the radio yet, she is doing well. Or even like Jimmy, a photographer for a naval ship off the coast of Africa. His pictures are in magazines all over the world.

I remembered a talk I had with Mama about how sometimes I envy others.

"There are people that envy you too, Sippy. There are people who would love to have your love for life and the ability to turn any situation good. You have a light in you, dear daughter, that not many possess. You see the good. Even right now, when you are venting, as you call it, you are only lookin' for the good. Don't lose that. Even I am jealous of it."

"Oh, Mama. I can't believe that. Any good in me came from you. Any good I have you have too."

"See what I mean, Sippy? You always find the good."

As I thought of that talk, I looked at all the good in my life. I thought of Jilly.

I remembered her many lessons. That's when I realized I knew in my heart my life was just how I wanted it. I knew I have spent all my life doing what I loved more than anything, and that was taking care of my kids, being with my friends and family, and experiencing love in ways most people only read about.

And then I knew, just like many years before, I needed to go to Alabama.

CHAPTER TWENTY-THREE

IT had been almost fifteen years since I had seen Jilly. She hadn't traveled for a long time. In fact, she put the old bike away a few years back, and she had hired part-time nurses to stay with her at home. She had nurses 24/7 before moving to the nursing home just before Christmas.

I told my mama and daddy I was going, packed a bag for me and the refrigerator for the kids, and gave them a little spending money and the "no parties while I'm gone speech." Then I left for my thirteen-hour journey to Bryan, Alabama.

I stopped just outside of town for gas and a Dr. Pepper. I decided I was hungry and was going to get a sandwich from the deli I thought they had. But there was no deli, so I just grabbed a pizza out of the warmer. I thought of Jilly when it ended up being the best pizza I have ever eaten.

I stopped for the night at the last stop in Missouri. I thought it sounded like a fun town, but I didn't see a darn thing that made it special. It had a cool name though. I can't remember it now, but it was cool. That is just some of that "don't judge a book by its cover" stuff.

I thanked God for life and a safe trip as I drifted off to a great sleep.

I woke early and had hotel coffee. And I finished off the pizza. It was even good ice-cold.

I went through Memphis again. It had a darkness about it. There was a sadness it didn't have thirty years ago. Buildings were boarded up. Trash lie along the highway. I didn't see any skyscrapers. I was trying to find Graceland.

I expected, after all these years, for it to be glorious with glitz and glamour. I started thinking I must have taken the wrong road. I wondered why Elvis would pick a place like this to live. I mean, he was Elvis!

I kept on the road that promised me Graceland. I saw Elvis everywhere, and I thought it sad how people capitalized on the man's death. Elvis Tires. Elvis Deli. Everything Elvis.

But no glitz. No bright lights. The buildings looked old for the most part, and many were abandoned or condemned. I was stunned. Out loud I voiced my disbelief, "I can't believe Elvis lived in the ghetto."

I think I laughed for ten minutes after that. I didn't mean it literally. But for the first time, I really understood that song. I was still laughing when I saw Graceland.

I was in awe at the sight and everything around me. I pulled into a small shopping center, and suddenly it all became clear. He was just a normal guy. And he wanted to live with real people. I had lunch there. I shopped at a few of the places in the square. The nicest people I have ever met were there. They made me feel comfortable. They smiled when I walked in, and they thanked me when I walked out. It was a great place.

I didn't tour Graceland. I just looked from the outside. I stood right by the gate I saw so many years ago. I decided I would come again another day. With the kids. I took pictures. I left Memphis with a happy heart. It was a beautiful place to me by the time I left.

I arrived in Bryan late. I went to Jilly's home, and I let myself in with the key hidden in the flowerpot outside. Everything was exactly as I remembered. Nothing had changed except for the old radio in the kitchen. It had been replaced with a modern stereo system.

It was probably the only new thing in the house except for an empty wheelchair and an array of medicine bottles and health care products. Seeing everything, I realized just how long it had been.

The remainder of a birthday celebration lay on the counter. The seven and three candles lay there with burnt wicks. I touched the outline of them and wished I could have been here in August to help her celebrate. Maybe next year, I thought. There was a note on the table. It was obviously written by one of Jilly's southern helpers. It was simple and to the point.

Dearest Serendipity,

There is food in the icebox. Help yourself. Miss Jilly is anxious to see you. She said to put the journals from the bedroom armoire in your car. They are yours now. I will call you tomorrow to see if you need anything.

Nurse Camilla

I took a shower and found the journals. There were fifteen in total. She had written in them every day of her life since 1963. I felt honored to have them. I decided not to start reading but to save them for another time.

I toured around the house, touching everything along my way. It was surreal to be there again after all those years. I realized my mother and father had touched this very wood, and the porch was the one they sat on. These weren't obvious observations when I had been here so many years before.

There were photos I actually took the time to look at, and I was amazed at the life in the eyes that stared back at me. I felt complete and at home. And now, for the first time, I have words to explain what I saw.

The old wood floors creaked as I walked. The house had a warmth that came from the books lining the walls inside the front door, and I touched each one as I walked by them. The blended smell of leather and wood was deep and strong. It added to the warmth I already felt. An oversized coat-tree, a mirrored armoire, and all the bookcases were hand-carved with intricate detail. The doorways with original, unpainted woodwork were inviting me to enter.

I went into the dining room where a table to seat ten dominated the center of the room. Captain's chairs were at each end. On the left wall was a swinging door for long-ago servants to enter through, and on the right was a curio cabinet of rich mahogany with shelves made of the thickest glass.

On those shelves were silver goblets, sparkling crystal wine glasses, and silver serving trays with floral patterns etched perfectly along their borders.

A buffet holding the finest china took up most of the far wall, and above it was a portrait of a man with light eyes and a beard. He was the head of the family—one of the grandfathers Jilly told me about. His eyes were kind, and he smiled slightly as if to approve my entrance into the house.

The fireplace mantle held the family clock. Its pendulum was still swinging with a precise rhythm. It reminded me of Jilly with a big piece of bubble gum in her mouth. I chuckled at the visual.

I walked on through and into the parlor. The parlor, where long ago I envisioned a man in a top hat, was now home to memories of Jilly and me. We spent hours curled up on that sofa with its floral pattern nestled under us. The faint light from the princess lamp on the table next to the sofa sent out a yellow glow that made the room even softer.

The telephone stand that still held a rotary dial phone was in the corner; the seat was worn, no doubt from Jilly as a teen, talking to possible suitors.

She talked to me about that—her life as a teen, that is. Those talks won't be shared here. Some things are only important to Jilly and me.

On the mantel was a statue of two bodies with no faces. I could hear the music they were dancing to, their bodies entwined in an unbreakable embrace. Next to it, a vase of purple with gold embossing looked heavy. I didn't lift it to check.

And above the fireplace was that painting. The one that touched me so long ago. It still did. I looked up at it before I left the room. It was still as real as ever. As I turned to leave, I swear that little girl waved. I smiled, but I didn't look back.

I went to sleep in the same bed I had slept on years before, and I had another talk with God.

"Hi. It's me. This bed is still as comfortable as ever. Thank you so much for this life. Thank you for this family and this heritage I have grown to appreciate so much. Thank you for being with me on my journey.

"And thank you for Jilly. Thank you with all my heart for her! Oh, and that pizza yesterday? Great! Really great! OK. Good night."

I slept better than I ever had.

CHAPTER TWENTY-FOUR

I spent a week in Bryan, Alabama. I went to the nursing home every day and Jilly and I talked about family and retold old stories. It was a great week, and she was happy. She was still beautiful. Her blonde hair had long turned white, and she kept it short now. It was thin, and so was she. But her eyes still had that sparkle, and that smile could still light up the room.

She had come to terms with her disease. She didn't like it none; don't get me wrong. She had plenty to say about that.

"I'm crippled, and I'm mad. But this place is nice." She smiled and giggled at herself, and she winked. "Great pizza!"

It had been a great week, and I didn't want it to end. But I had to go home. I loaded my car with my bag, some snacks I had bought the night before, and Jilly's journals. I wore a new shirt I found at a flea market on the edge of town. I wore it for Jilly. I added her old, beaded necklace, and I was ready to go.

I left a note on the table for her helpers thanking them for taking such good care of her. I took one last look at the house. Her care was expensive, and I knew she would have to sell it soon.

"See ya later," I said to the quiet as I let myself out.

I stopped at the nursing home on my way out of Bryan. There were only a few people roaming around the garden out front. The inside of the lobby was welcoming. It was like a home. There was a sitting area, complete with a television, and a baby grand piano. The plants decorating the corners and tables were real and gave it warmth.

There wasn't that musty smell some facilities have. It wasn't medicinal. It smelled of pine, but it wasn't like Pine-Sol, thank goodness. No, it smelled of pine trees. I suspected it to be a remaining candle from the Christmas holiday last month. I liked it, and it made me feel calm.

I called the elevator to take me up to the third floor. I shared it with a patient and the aide that was helping him. He wasn't old. He was probably my age, but he was in a wheelchair. I wondered what had happened to him. He smiled at me when I stepped on the elevator.

They were talking about music. He was talking about KISS being the best rock band ever, and she was teasing him to get out of the 80s. He laughed at her. It was a real laugh from his heart. She laughed with him. I could tell he was more than a patient to her. And she was more than a nurse to him. I let them leave the elevator ahead of me, and I held the door as his nurse patiently waited for him to control his electric chair.

It was hard for him, and I thought how much easier it would have been for her to just do it. But then I saw how he loved the independence. It was important to him. She praised him as he made it through the door without scraping the sides of it.

"You're getting awful good at that, Kevin," she said. "High-five!"

She waited while he got his better arm in the air to slap hers. He smiled up at her. They were friends. Good friends. I couldn't help but smile. It made me feel good to know there were nurses like that there.

I got to Jilly's room, and her journal was lying heavy on her knees. I stood in the doorway and watched her sleep. I remembered so much of our life together.

Silly Jilly. I remembered watching fireworks in fifteen degree weather. We were bundled up in some old coveralls and gloves we found in the basement. We took cocoa with us, and we sat on the hood of her old car to watch them. She cried at how pretty they were.

"Cryin' ain't just for being sad, Serendipitay. It's for all the time. Tears take up space, so ya need to make room every now and again!"

I remembered the hats and her bike. How she got those old hats out and started wearing them.

"Jilly, those hats are forty years old. You must look so silly!"

"Well, I may look silly, but I'm not sweatin' like all those fools laughin' at me. Alabama sun is a scorcher, ya know!"

I thought about how much she loved pizza and how excited she got when I made her a cheeseburger one. She laughed and laughed that I put the Big Mac recipe on a pizza crust.

She sang the jingle as she doubled-checked if I remembered everything. Of course, she changed "sesame bun" to "this here pizza crust."

I remembered how she sent me flowers in '94 when John Lennon and Sir Elton made it into the Rock and Roll Hall of Fame. She called it my victory. And I remembered how she laughed and took it all back last year when her beloved Ramones got the honor. She said there weren't enough flowers for me to send her.

Smiling at the memories of her, I walked slowly into her room. She looked so calm. Her eyes were closed while she napped. Her journal was there, open. She had written as eloquently as ever. I read what she wrote:

This is my last entry, as my eyes are no longer working well enough to see. My writing must look like chicken scratch on this old paper. My heart and mind are good as ever, but my thoughts and body are tired. The sky is clear today. There is a breeze. The trees outside my window sway some. I will have a visitor later. My brother's child. His little Sippy, but whom I call Serendipity. It's such a beautiful name. This journal will go to her with all the others. I bought her a journal of her own. I will give it to her today. She will finish my beginning …

And at the bottom of the page she wrote:

> *To my Dearest Serendipity,*
> *You have the best of your father in you—his physical beauty and a searching mind. You have talents in music and the ability to meet people with ease. You have a gift. The spirit guides will support you with their strengths if you seek them to use that gift. Listen to the voice, child. It knows, and so will you.*
> *Love always and forever, Jilly.*

As I finished reading over her shoulder, she looked up at me. She smiled. We sat for a bit in silence. I held her hand. Then we talked for a while. We laughed. We shared more memories. We talked about my drive home. She told me to be careful, and I said I would.

"What do we do now?" she asked, although did not wait for an answer. "This is not the end," she continued. "No! This is not the end!"

"No, it's not. I will come to see you again. In the summer, I will come again."

"Don't say good-bye," she said and chuckled. "See ya later. Say see ya later."

She told me she loved me, and she handed me a package she had tucked under her blanket.

I unwrapped it carefully. Inside was a pink leather journal. It was empty of words but filled with love. It was the most beautiful gift I had ever been given. She looked up, and her eyes were tired, indeed, but they still smiled.

I leaned down, kissed her, and she drifted off to sleep.

"OK. See ya later."

It came out as a whisper. I couldn't talk. I couldn't swallow.

"I love you, Aunt Jilly," I said in my mind.

I left her room and walked down the hall. Kevin and his nurse were still talking about music. She promised to bring him a CD of good stuff. I smiled again at their friendship, and I knew Jilly would be well taken care of.

I walked out into the brisk January air. I sat on a nearby bench and looked at the two books she had given me. First was her journal. It was old and weathered. There were many like it in the trunk of my car. I would cherish them. And then there was the new one—the journal she had given me. I was about to open it when a voice said, "Great shirt!"

I looked up to see a man walking toward me. He was pointing to the Ramones shirt I had worn in honor of Jilly.

"Oh, thanks. They're one my aunt's favorite bands," I said as I pointed toward the building. "She was a bit of a hippy in her day."

I smiled at him. He smiled back.

"Serendipity?" he said as a question and a salutation. He smiled then and bore a striking resemblance to John Cusack.

"Yeah?" I said as an obvious question.

"I'm Book McCann. Your aunt knows my mom and dad, While and Linda," he said with odd enthusiasm. He continued, smiling. "So you are Serendipity? Like the movie?"

"Well, yes. But not after the movie. And everybody calls me Sippy. Just Sippy."

He had begun to walk away toward the building, but he spun around. While he continued to walk, he went forward then backwards.

"Serendipity. It's one of my favorite words!"

He almost had to yell, as he was close to the building. He continued to smile. With that, he turned around and disappeared inside. I heard him whistle as the door closed behind him.

At that moment, butterflies stirred in my stomach, and that was it. I knew. There was no doubt. I gave God a quick thumbs-up and turned to the book in my lap. I opened the journal Jilly had given me. The inscription inside was simple.

Write it all down, Serendipity. Don't leave anything out. Tell
a good story!
Love, Jilly

I took out a pen, and with the greatest love I have ever felt, I made my first journal entry.

"Never have been good at tellin' stories. Mama says I talk too fast … "